A Trip to the Lake with Kim

Dirk Caldwell Romantic Erotic Novels, Volume 4

Dirk Caldwell

Published by Dirk Caldwell, 2023.

A TRIP TO THE LAKE WITH KIM

First edition. July 17, 2023.

ISBN: 979-8223825821

Written by Dirk Caldwell.

Also by Dirk Caldwell

Adventures of Stan
Stan Does a Big Girl and Gives her a Big Orgasm
Stan Does a Female Police Officer While On Duty
Stan Scores on a Booty Call with Barbara
Stan Takes Barb's Anal Cherry
Stan Teaches Oklahoma Karen About Sex in the City
Stan gets Kinky with Barb on Vacation
Barb Wants more Orgasms with Stan before She gets Engaged to Another Man
Stan Does Barbara's Mom!
Stan Titty Fucks Barbara's Friend!
A Stopover in Eufaula to Fuck Lynn Again
Stan Shows a Redhead How to Have an Orgasm
Liz loses Her Anal Cherry During a Three Way
Stan has Sex with a Black Chick!
Stan Has Sex with a Pregnant Woman!
Stan Sport Fucks a Sexy Lawyer!
Stan Titty Fucks Traci's Grandma!
Stan Titty Fucks His Art Dealer!

Dirk Caldwell Romantic Erotic Novels
A Visit to the Farm with Darla - a Sexy Short Story

A Layover in Omaha with Tina
A Night in Eufaula with Lynn
A Trip to the Lake with Kim
Older Women need Love, too! Erika visits Atlanta
Lessons in Love: Gabriella Visits Indianapolis
Big Girls Need Love, too! Barbara from Kokomo
Flight Attendants want Love: Flying High with Jessica
Back to the Farm with Darla - A Sexy Sequel
Redheads Need Love: Megan From New Orleans
A Big Girl finds Love: Joann from Shreveport
Lust from London: My Affair with a British Nymphomaniac
Paula's Sexy European Weekend
Mother and Daughter Threesome

Dirk Caldwell Sexy Short Stories
To All the Girls I've Loved Before: Sexy Short Stories Book 1
To All the Girls I've Loved Before: Sexy Short Stories Book 2
To All the Girls I've Loved Before: Sexy Short Stories Book 3

Table of Contents

Acknowledgment

Cover image by Lyashenko on Freepik

Introduction

I held Kim by her slippery waist as I moved my rigid cock into her pussy while she groaned. We had been riding my jet ski and the sexual tension got high as the fighter pilot in her took over and she guided us through some wild maneuvers as she drove the jet ski like it was a fighter plane. Excited, we stopped in a quiet cove, hopped off and got naked in the water, and well, things happened after she stroked my cock.

I moved into her as she faced me and began a fast thrusting rhythm as she held me tightly and moaned. I would be coming soon, into an Air Force officer and fellow airline pilot. I imagined that was against the rules in some manual somewhere, but a hard dick has no conscience as they say.

My name is Dirk. Well, that's not my real name. I'd never be able to have a normal life if I used my real name. I was an airline pilot and single at the time of this encounter. I enjoyed being unencumbered and the benefits that came from that. I could travel the world as an international aircrew member and be with any woman I wanted without regret and have always enjoyed the freedom that came with that ability.

While I love writing about my encounters, I always change enough of the information about the ladies so my writing could not possibly be traced back to them. Cities are changed, along with names, occupations, specific characteristics, branches of service for the military, etc. To do otherwise would not be gentlemanly. I do, however, mix in some of my local knowledge about locations. How did I get that information? Let your imagination be your guide.

I hope you enjoy this story.

Meeting up with Kim

I had briefly met Kim a few weeks before at the flight deck door of an airliner as I was deadheading from Omaha back to Atlanta. She and I passed very closely, and we both felt a spark of interest, maybe more. She had pressed her boobs up against my chest as she passed by me, so I was very intrigued by her. We had traded phone numbers at the time of the encounter and then spent some time coordinating a time and place to meet. I was very interested in her, and it seemed she had the same curiosity.

It's hard to date another pilot. Our schedules are complex, and this particular month-long schedule, which we call a bid, was not conducive to a meeting, even for a dinner date. I was on a schedule going back and forth to Europe on her days off, and she was on reserve or on-call duty on my days off. We tried to meet on one of her reserve days, but she got called out to fly.

I thought of what I knew about her so far. She was tall, almost my height, attractive, with shoulder-length brown hair that I had seen in a ponytail thus far. She was slender and athletic looking and had the prettiest green eyes. I knew this from a very close look into them from a few inches away during our brief encounter. She was looking directly into mine as well. I had found out she was an Air Force veteran, like me. Unlike me, she was an officer and a pilot, flying the F-16 fighter. She seemed sassy and smart. I wondered what she would think when she found out I was a former Air Force enlisted guy. If we ever got a chance to meet, that is. I was looking forward to seeing her again, very much. I had that feeling that there would be a sexual encounter on the first date.

The new bid schedule came out, and we talked on the phone soon after. The scheduling gods had smiled upon us, and we both had a very unusual four-day break at the same time in the first week of the new bid. After discussion, we agreed to meet on the first of the four days off.

"

I think we were both thinking that if things worked out, we would have several days to, you know ... hang out together. Or perhaps more.

We talked again a few days later and confirmed meeting up on a Tuesday. We talked about logistics because pilots are planners, and she said parking was awful around her apartment, so I should park at an outlying station, and take Atlanta's excellent MARTA train system to her stop. Her apartment was only a few blocks from the station, and she said there were lots of eating places around her apartment within walking distance. That sounded fine to me, I usually took MARTA to work to avoid traffic hassles and was very familiar with the system.

I was flying a trip to Frankfurt and back just before our date, getting back the Monday afternoon the day prior to our meeting. If all went well, I would have a confirmed date with a tall, pretty girl the day after I got back. I left for Germany on Saturday afternoon with a spring in my step and a smile on my face. My Captain kept asking me why I was smiling.

I arrived back in Atlanta on time on Monday afternoon, which is a small miracle in itself. As soon as I turned my phone on, I saw that I had a text and a voicemail from Kim. I hoped it was not a cancellation, and I read the text carefully as we walked toward customs. It read:

"Dirk! I am getting back from a trip Monday early afternoon. If you get in on time, let's meet tonight instead of waiting until tomorrow. Let me know! Kim."

It was very good news and made good sense to me. I stopped very quickly and sent a reply:

"Tonight it is! Going through customs right now. Send me the time you want me to pick you up at the apartment."

The entire crew was waiting for me impatiently. We had to go through customs as a group, and I was holding up the process. I said, "Sorry!" and we all resumed.

The Purser was walking next to me, and teased, "Coordinating a date, Dirk?"

"How did you know?" I smiled.

"Because you have an even bigger grin on your face than you have had this entire trip. Enjoy!"

My phone beeped as soon as we passed through customs. It was Kim:

"1900 at my place, please. Does that give you enough time?"

The time was adequate for me to head back to my condo, clean up, and make the trip to her place. I sent back an acknowledgment and hurried to operations to stow my kit bag, sign out from the trip, and head home. My phone beeped again. She had sent a smiley face.

At the condo, I showered, shaved, and dressed in one of my nicest polo shirts, nice shorts with a belt, and my usual loafers with no socks. I hesitated for a moment, then sprinkled a little baby powder on my chest from a travel-sized bottle a nice lady had given me the month before, the same day I met Kim, as a matter of fact. Kim had commented that day we met on the scent of the baby powder that the nice lady had rubbed into my chest hair. I hoped it drove her wild.

I had no trouble finding the apartment and it was almost exactly 1900 when I knocked on the door. She opened it within a few seconds, and I was taken aback at how good she looked. Her brown hair was brushed out and down. I had not imagined her in anything but the ponytail. She was wearing a nice collared bright floral print blouse, tucked into very short white shorts, accentuating her long, tanned athletic legs. She wore just a minimum of eye makeup. She had nice white sandals on, as well as a gold necklace and a tennis bracelet. Her big pilot-style watch was on her left wrist, and she did not have any rings on her fingers that had conservatively cut nails with clear polish.

We looked at each other for a moment, smiling. I said something dumb like, "We meet again!"

She laughed, and said, "You are the hardest person to get together with. I'm glad our schedules worked out. Come in!"

We went in and stood inside the door. She said, "I made up some margaritas out of a frozen mix, it's in the blender. Would you like one before we head out?"

"That sounds great, Kim. Thanks."

I followed her to the small kitchen and watched her work the blender, and then took the glass she offered. We each said, "Cheers!"

"To pilots on their days off!"

She smiled. "Agreed! Now let's sit down and visit."

We sat on the sofa, and she drew her long legs up, turned towards me, and looked into my eyes with her pretty green ones. I looked back. It took a moment for me to say something.

"I remember those eyes."

She smiled in return. "Thanks, and I remember the scent of baby powder. Do you always wear it?"

I almost blushed. "No, I remembered you saying you liked the smell of it during our brief encounter in Omaha."

"I'm flattered that you remembered that. I got a hell of a feeling about you when I squeezed by you that day. Ever since then, I've been wanting to see what that was about."

"Me, too."

She smiled again. "Tell me all about yourself, Dirk."

"Well, I grew up in California. Typical suburban childhood. Dad was an engineer for IBM. After high school, I joined the Air Force and started out as a mechanic, then cross-trained to boom operator ..."

She interrupted me excitedly. "That is so cool! I wonder if you ever refueled me. Can I call you Boomer?"

"You may. I might have refueled you; I certainly have done my share of F-16s. You never know. I was on the KC-135, then went to the KC-10 in its infancy, then finished my career in Louisiana. I found out that my wearing glasses was not a restriction to getting hired any longer with the airlines, so I went to a big flight school here in Atlanta, got all my ratings, built hours doing flight instruction for a couple of years, then flew for a commuter airline, then a small major airline, then eventually got on here." I paused. "Flying for this airline has been a dream of mine since I can remember."

She shook her head. "Damn, Dirk. That is one hell of a career path. You guys with a civil background have to get a lot more flying hours to get looked at than us military guys. Where do you live, around here?"

"I have a condo up I-85 in Norcross that is my home of record, but I usually spend most of the summer on a houseboat on Lake Lanier."

She laughed. "Get out! That is so cool! Am I going to be able to see your boat?"

That made me smile. "That depends on how this first date goes. You may run away screaming."

"I don't think we are in any danger of that. We still have to figure out that mutual feeling."

We were about finished with our drinks. She looked at her watch. "Shall we go to dinner, and I will tell you my life story on the way there? I'm hungry!"

We got up and went down to the main street. After a short discussion, she wanted to try an Ethiopian place nearby. We walked along, with her long legs making it easy to walk next to her. She filled me in on her history.

"I come from a Marine Corps family. Dad did 30 years and got out as a Master Gunnery Sergeant. I have two brothers, I'm the oldest. We traveled all over the world, and I was in probably 10 different schools. After high school, we were in San Diego. I applied for and got a full-ride ROTC scholarship at UC Berkeley." She laughed. "Dad was pretty pissed at me for going to such a liberal school. But they needed more women students, and it was a pretty easy program. We didn't even have to wear our uniforms around campus so we would not offend the communists. Then I got picked up for a pilot training slot, did well there, and got my first choice which was the F-16. I wasn't even close to being the first female fighter pilot, so that was easier."

I asked, "How did the male fighter jocks treat you?"

"It was about 50/50 guys trying to get in my pants or treat me like a sister. About what I expected. Here we are."

We went in, and soon we placed a drink order for another round of margaritas while we looked at the menu. She asked, "You flew with women in the tanker, right?"

"Yeah, they started showing up in 1980, navigators first, then the first few copilots. Most of them were just fine, a few were on an ego trip, and a few were kind of activists about women's pilot's rights and seemed like they were seeking publicity."

We decided on appetizers rather than dinner. Ethiopian appetizers were as interesting as the girl across from me.

I looked at her. "So, margaritas go with Ethiopian food?"

"I have no idea. They must, or they would not serve them here."

"Your logic is not sound."

"I can see we are about to have our first disagreement. Anyway, I am still flying the F-16 for the Guard. I am a brand new Major in the Georgia Air National Guard."

"Congratulations!"

"Thanks. I didn't really have to do anything; they had an open slot and I fit the time in grade as a Captain and the other qualifications." We heard some music start, slow and jazzy. It was a DJ thing in the corner. She said, "Ooohh. There's a dance floor. Let's dance!"

"I, ah ..."

"C'mon, Boomer!" She was halfway to the floor. I had no choice.

First dance

We were the only dancers, if you can call what I do dancing. Kind of controlled shuffling. We started out with one arm around each other, holding one hand up, with pelvises a discrete distance apart. After a minute, she said, "Ah, this is like high school. Come closer!" and put her arms around my neck. I was a little surprised, then put my arms around her. She pulled me a little closer. "There we go, that's better!"

We swayed together to the music, in an enjoyable embrace. I had both arms full of a tall, firm, warm, good-smelling, pretty girl. It was heavenly. After a minute, she pulled me even closer, then moved her head and looked me in the eyes. Her nose was about a quarter inch from mine. I was feeling that spark again. Her lips were in the right spot, and it seemed like the thing to do, so I kissed her for about five seconds on the lips.

When I pulled back, her eyes were closed, and her lips parted. Then her eyes opened, and I stared into a pool of green, mesmerized. She looked back at me for a moment, then put a hand behind my neck and pulled me to her mouth. This time, our tongues explored each other and intertwined hungrily. I felt as if my soul was on fire, and we had merged at the molecular level. Sometime during that, she pulled me into her hard, and I could feel her hips move against me. I don't know if we kissed for 10 seconds or 10 minutes, but when we came up for air, she was looking at me with her eyes wide open, and her mouth whispered, "Holy shit!"

As we came to our senses, it seemed we had an audience. Some other diners were clapping, and some whistled. Embarrassed, we both headed back to our seats. "Smile and wave, boomer. Smile and wave." She waved and called out, "First date, folks! Just getting to know each other!" We heard chuckles from some of the other diners.

We sat down, chagrined. We looked at each other. She was the first to speak.

"Damn, boomer! What the hell was that?"

I took a sip of my drink. "I'd say we are attracted to each other like we first thought back in Omaha."

"Attracted? Attracted? Hell, we are 30 minutes into our first date, and I was dry-humping you on the dance floor in front of all of Atlanta!" She put her face in her hands. "What the hell is happening?"

I tried to be kind. "In all fairness, it's more like an hour. Besides, we have known each other for two weeks or so."

She looked up, then leaned over. "Dirk? I'm flushed, and very turned on. Did you drug me or something? Just who the hell are you?"

"Negative on the drugs. I'm just a regular guy that is very attracted to you."

"I should say so." She downed the rest of her drink and fanned her face with the dessert menu. "I need another. As long as I am going to have your children, you may as well tell me more about yourself."

The food arrived as she was finishing her proclamation, and the server was kind of flustered by it. Kim asked the server sweetly, "Can you bring the father of my children and me another margarita, please? Thank you." The server nodded vigorously and almost ran away.

"Father of your children?"

"That's right. I have never felt anything like that pure sexual urge. Besides, the talk of fatherhood probably helped your boner subside, right?"

"That it did."

She smiled. "Shall we eat? Suddenly I am ravenous after you were groping me on the dance floor."

"Groping you? I'm sorry, Major. That was you who stuck your tongue down my throat."

She chewed a bite of appetizer. "While that is technically accurate, it was you who started the kiss thing."

She had me there. "I've wanted to kiss you since you rubbed your boobs on me on the airplane in Omaha."

She smiled. "That feeling was mutual. Please excuse me for dry humping you. That's very unladylike."

"You are forgiven. I can't call you Major. Do you have one of those cool fighter call signs?"

She laughed. "Unfortunately, all they could come up with was 'Kimbo.' Like bimbo."

"Kim it is in that case."

"Please continue with all relevant personal details. Wives? Kids?"

"One wife, a long time ago, no kids. Not looking to start anything long-term. You?"

She sighed. "Kind of the same, except no husbands, don't really want kids. I love my nieces and nephews. My long-term goal is to be happy, have great sex, and see the world."

I raised my glass. "I'll drink to that." We clinked glasses.

I had to ask something. "Kim? Are you okay with the officer/enlisted relationship thing?"

She had the answer already. "I thought about that as we were walking over here. Since you are not currently serving, it's not a problem. Besides, I think it's delightfully naughty to be screwing an enlisted man."

I laughed. "Are you going to be screwing an enlisted man?"

"Oh, Yeah! You can count on that, and the sooner the better. For a moment there, I was going to be clearing the table and doing you right here!"

"We'd probably get another round of applause."

"No, we'd probably get arrested, and that would not do our careers any good with our very conservative employer."

After finishing the drinks and appetizers, it was time to change venues. We argued about who was paying and agreed to split the check. A bit tipsy, we stepped out into the warm Georgia night and started walking slowly back along the street to her place when she grabbed my hand and pulled me to the doorway of a closed shop. She turned to me, put her arms around me, and looked into my eyes, then our mouths came together in mutual agreement. We kissed for a few minutes standing there, and then, out of breath, we continued down the street.

She said, "Well, that attraction is still there. Wow."

"Wow indeed. You're a hell of a kisser."

"Thanks, you're not bad yourself. I'm kind of wound up again. I'm ready to take you back to my place and get started. Oh, look! There's a karaoke place! Let's go in."

Karaoke, Korean Style

She had the attention span of a squirrel and was already heading in. I was learning that with Kim there was going to be some catching up whenever a new idea sprouted. We went into the dimly lit venue and found a table. She decided shots of tequila were in order, and I insisted on a beer chaser for both of us. A person came by and handed us a big, multi-page karaoke song list and slips of paper to write our choice on. We were to write our song choices on the slip of paper and take them to the DJ, who would call out the name of the next singer.

I looked around at the clientele, then the song list, then the DJ. "Kim? Have you noticed something different about this place?"

"Not really, why?"

"Everyone in here except us is Asian."

"So?"

"And the song list is in Korean. And the DJ looks Korean."

She looked around and looked at the song list and the DJ, who had the first singer starting yowling in a foreign language.

"Shit! We're in a Korean karaoke bar!"

We both burst out laughing as the drinks came. The waitress said, in heavily accented English, "I get you English song list!"

We toasted and sipped our tequila and listened to Korean singing. The language of Korea is not always pleasant to Western ears, and we were gamely hanging on when the English song list came. It was on one page and did not have a lot of variety. We looked it over.

"Here, boomer. You have a deep voice, do some Sinatra! Here, I'll sign you up for 'New York, New York!" She filled out a slip and carried it up to the DJ, who smiled and put it in the pile of slips.

"Okay, Kim, how's your Linda Ronstadt? Blue Bayou has your name all over it." I did the same, filled out a slip for her, and dropped it off. "Now, let's finish these drinks and haul ass before they call our names."

We were not that lucky.

Soon the DJ called out, "Mister Dirk? Please come to podium to sing, "New York, New York." I glared at Kim, who was clapping.

I went to the podium, took the microphone, and in a margarita and tequila-induced fit of bravado, belted out the song with considerable feeling as Kim clapped along. The audience of Koreans was silent during my performance. As I concluded, the audience erupted in loud applause and cheering in Korean. At least I thought it was cheering. I went back to the table, where Kim stood and kissed me. I waved to the crowd and sat down.

Kim said, "That was great, boomer! I had no idea you could sing!"

"Neither could I, Kim. Neither could I."

Several audience members came over and enthusiastically thanked me, and several shooters of tequila magically appeared on the table. Kim laughed, "You're a hit!"

Things calmed down, and we thought it rude not to drink the shooters, so as we worked through them, the songs in Korean continued. The more tequila we drank, the less we minded the caterwauling in Korean.

Then the DJ announced, "Miss Kimbo? Please come to the podium to sing, "Broo Bayoo." Or at least that's what it sounded like. Kim replied to me, "Oh shit, boomer! I can't sing!"

"You can now. Do it for the Georgia Air Guard!" She gave me the finger, but marched to the podium, thanked the DJ for the microphone, and cut loose. It was a very good rendition, ending with her head thrown back, a hand in the air, and carrying the last high note to the end. The crowd went wild! A great majority of them came over, shook both our hands, thanked Kim profusely, and dropped more shooters on the table.

I hugged Kim. "You were great, Kimbo!" she laughed shyly and sat down after waving to the crowd.

"It's amazing the false courage you get after a few shots. Where the hell did these come from? I thought we were done!"

"They are from your fan club. Drink up."

We made a valiant effort at putting the tequila away. It was getting very drunk out. Just when we thought we were done, a contingent of fans came over and said, "Please, Sir. Sing New York again. Please?"

I protested mightily, and Kim was no help, "C'mon boomer! One more time!" Then the group said, "Both, please." And indicated both of us. I had to laugh.

"A duet?" The group nodded happily. Kim looked aghast. "Okay, but no more drinks, please. Thank You!" I took Kim by the hand and led her somewhat unsteadily to the podium, where the smiling DJ handed us both microphones. We smiled at each other, and the music began.

We belted out New York like Sinatra would have, with gusto and feeling. When we finished the last note in a dramatic fashion, the crowd exploded in applause and cheering. We walked back to our table, and I leaned to Kim and said, "Grab your purse! We are outa here!" She grabbed it on the way by and we made our exit, waving and shaking hands like it was a political rally. We made it out the door, looked at each other, and started laughing our asses off.

Outside the karaoke place, we walked as steadily as we could for half a block, then Kim said, "Boomer, I have to sit down. I'm dizzy."

I found a bus stop bench not too far away and aimed us for it. We plopped down, and she leaned into me. "Oh, boomer. I'm so wasted. Can you get us to my apartment?"

Assuring her that I could navigate, we waited out her bout of dizziness and set off in the correct direction. After a few blocks, it all started looking familiar, and with some difficulty found ourselves at her door. We fumbled with the key for a bit, then were finally inside. I walked her to the bathroom and hoped she would not be sick.

Back at the apartment

Kim came out after a while, and we decided we should sit down before we fell down. I had not been that drunk in a long time but was doing better than she was. She assured me that she would not be sick, but asked for some water, which I thought was a splendid idea. I got cold bottled water from the kitchen fridge and returned to find her swaying in the middle of the room. We made it to the sofa, and she crawled up to my lap.

Kim sat on my lap with her arms around my neck and we kissed for a couple of minutes as our hands roamed each other's bodies. She then said, "I'd like to have sex, but I think I'm too drunk to enjoy it. Can I have a rain gauge? Rain check? Whatever that is."

"I understand and will be happy to issue a rain check, redeemable for sex at any future date."

"Thanks, you're a doll." She nuzzled my neck. "This is nice, I can tell that even though I can't tell much else. Most men would have my shorts off and be banging my drunk ass by now."

"I always try to be a gentleman."

"You are indeed a fine example for mankind!" Then she started hiccupping.

"Hic! Oh shit, I have the hiccups." She alternated hiccupping and giggling for a while. Every time her body jerked while hiccupping, her hips would jerk, causing a movement that was quite stimulating as she sat crossways on my lap. My cock started to swell involuntarily. She soon noticed.

"Aw man, I'm sorry. You're getting a stiffy and I'm too drunk to fuck."

"That's okay, Kim. We'll make up for it later."

"Bullshit! I am going to take care of a fellow Air Force veteran right the fuck now!"

She scooted around so she was now straddling me, reached down, unzipped my shorts, and deftly pulled my semi-engorged dick out and commenced to pump it vigorously, all while hiccupping and giggling.

"How about a nice hand job? Will that be a suitable substitute for sex? Hic!"

I was enjoying the activity very much. What could I say? "Yep, that'll be fine until we can do it the right way."

"Cool!" she exclaimed and continued the pumping, now humming as she did so. It was very interesting.

After a few minutes of pumping, humming, hiccupping, and giggling, she announced, "This is boring!" swung off my lap, got on her knees on the floor between my legs, and put my dick in her mouth, starting an enthusiastic and noisy, slurping blow job, still occasionally hiccupping.

"Kim! I don't want to take advantage of you while you're drunk. Come on back up to my lap."

She pulled back and looked up at me, some saliva dripping from her mouth "No, it's cool. I am sort of knowing what I am doing, and it is curing the hiccups. Just don't come in my mouth, I might get sick."

I did an internal review of my ethics and morals. I had agreed not to fuck her while drunk, and she in turn had exchanged this for a hand job and a blow job. In my semi-buzzed state, I thought I was in the clear.

"Okay, I'll let you know when I am about to come."

She had resumed the sloppy blow job, and I thought heard her say okay, but the sound was somewhat muffled by the cock in her mouth. She did give me a thumbs-up signal without raising her head.

After a minute or two of noisy oral sex, she sat up and announced, "More stimulation is needed! We'll go with some visuals!" and then unbuttoned and stripped off her blouse, and tossed it aside. She then reached around her back and undid her bra, tossing that in the air. I thought it might catch the ceiling fan, but she missed it. She then raised her arms and said, "Ta-da! Behold my magnificent hooters!" and looked at me proudly with a grin on her face.

I was laughing. "You fighter pilots are all nut cases!"

"Yes, that is a given. Are you beholding my boobies? Behold!"

I admired her tits. She was about a 34B, a nice size to play with, and had nice tan lines from a small bikini. She had very long nipples, which always turned me on. Those would be fun to play with. "I have beheld your boobies. Very nice! Magnificent, even!"

"Thank you, thank you very much! I think they are great, too! You may touch them if you wish."

I did play with them for a minute, then she said, "Excuse me," and bent back over to continue the enthusiastic blow job. I saw one of her hands go into her shorts and she started fingering herself. The sight of all this was too much. Within a minute, biological back pressure was building in my balls, and ejaculation was imminent. "Kim, I'm about to come!" I gasped.

She pulled back with a plop as my cock exited her mouth, grabbed my dick, and started pumping rapidly. She knew her way around a dick, even when drunk! After about 30 seconds, I could feel the cum coming. "Here it comes!" I managed to blurt out.

Then she said, "Well shit! What are we going to do with that stuff?" She looked around for something to catch it with, shrugged, and pointed my dick at her naked chest. "This will have to do!"

I started laughing and coming at the same time, a first for me. A jet of hot cum shot over her tits and chest, followed by another, then a small last one. She was still pumping vigorously, while making encouraging remarks, like, "Yeah! Woo hoo!"

After a minute, she said, "All done? Offload complete as you tanker guys say?"

I was still laughing. "Offload completed. Stowing the boom."

"Roger! Oooh, there's still a little coming out." She reached up with a finger and wiped a stray dribble of cum off the end of my dick, then drunkenly looked at her finger with a few drops of cum on it. "Hmmm." She looked down at her chest and tits, covered with cum, shrugged, and put her finger in her mouth, licking it clean. She was insane!

"Not bad! I should have let you come in my mouth and saved all this mess. Shit!"

She reached for her blouse on the floor and started mopping up operations.

I protested, "That will stain that pretty blouse!" It was a gooey mess. She continued unabated, then tossed the blouse aside, wobbling on her knees a little.

I said, "Let's go get you cleaned up," and stood up and helped her up.

I led us into the bathroom, with her very unsteady on her feet. She sat down on the closed toilet lid as I found a washcloth, ran it under warm water, and used it to clean us both up. "Thanks! I gotta pee!" she announced, raised up, lifted the lid, dropped her shorts and panties, sat back down, and started peeing in one smooth motion. "Damn, I almost didn't make it."

I went back to the living room as she was peeing, looking around for debris. I took her sticky shirt into the laundry room and put it in the sink and ran cold water over it to keep it from staining. Back in the living room, I picked up her sandals and put them by the door. Then I found her bra in the corner and took it into the bedroom. She was lying in bed naked with the sheet pulled up about halfway over her. "I'm dizzy, so I thought I'd lie down. I don't feel sick right now, and don't want to barf."

"You should drink some water."

"I guess you're right. Do you mind bringing me some?"

I went back to the living room and found cool bottles of water. Taking it back to her, she sat up and drank it down. She looked at me. "You're still dressed. How about that? You have some drool or something around your zipper. Better wipe that off."

I did so in the bathroom and came back to the bed.

Looking up at me sleepily, she said, "I want you to cuddle with me. Can you spend the night?"

"I'd like that. I'm on days off, so we can sleep in."

"I am, too. Strip off and get in with me."

I undressed down to my underwear and laid my clothes on the dresser. I crawled into bed and scooted up to her and we spooned. I pulled her hair back and kissed the back of her neck.

She stirred sleepily. "Mmmmm. Nice. Dirk? Can we go to your houseboat tomorrow?"

"Sure. We'll work out the details when we get up tomorrow. Are you still dizzy?"

"Yeah, but it's not so bad when you hold me. Big tough fighter pilot, huh? I feel like a girl."

"Well, you are a girl. Although you are crazy, you are a lot of fun."

"Thanks. You can play with my boobs a little as we fall asleep. Don't finger me, though, I need to sleep."

"Yes, Ma'am!"

She chuckled a little. I took a free hand and gently ran them over her nice boobs, softly fondling them. I stayed away from the nipples, even though I really wanted to play with them. She was asleep almost immediately, with me following suit soon after.

Day One - Tuesday

We awoke at about the same time. I gave her a kiss, and we compared notes. I felt pretty rough but was functional. She groaned and said, "I feel like shit. How many shots did you make me do?"

"I made you do zero. You consumed between 2 and 10 shots of tequila."

"I admit to a certain degree of culpability. Crap. How do you feel?"

I admitted to not being 100 percent.

She then asked, "Can we still go to the lake?"

"Sure, we can get some supplies on the way and then be there by noon."

"Okay. Are we showering together?"

I smiled. "That would be nice, but only in a platonic manner."

"You are so full of shit. Okay, after I pee, we can shower."

We had a quick shower, each washing the other off. Although it was very nice, we did not feel up to shower sex, so it was over quickly.

She dressed in a different pair of short shorts, athletic shoes, and a tee shirt that said, "Remove before flight." Nice touch. I dressed in what I had on the night before.

She then asked, "How long are we going to the boat for?"

I pondered that. "If we are having a good time, three nights, four days. If we are not having a good time, I will put you on a bus back here at any time."

"Fair enough." She got an empty Air Force helmet bag out of her closet. "Let's see. Two or three swimsuits, two or three tee shirts, a couple of pairs of shorts. Flip flops. Should I take underwear?"

"Yes, I think so."

"Are we going anywhere nice? Do I need to take something else?"

I thought for a minute. "No, everywhere around there is pretty casual."

"I'll toss something semi-nice in just in case."

She threw some girl stuff in the bag, like a toothbrush, some makeup, hair scrunchies, and a hairbrush. "Good to go, GI!"

She was a trip. "You are the fastest-packing woman I have ever seen."

"Of course! Let's go."

We walked to the MARTA station and waited for a train. She leaned into me and moaned. "Oh fuck, just shoot me. I feel crappy."

"Okay, I have a gun in my truck. I'll shoot you then."

"Thanks, you're a peach. Did I really let you come on my boobs last night? I sort of remember that."

"Yes, you did and it was a moment of splendor."

She sighed. "Glad you enjoyed it. Can I go back to sleep now?"

"No, first we must eat."

She made a face. "I don't think that is a good idea."

"Oh yes, I have a plan."

We got on a train, and she leaned on me as we rode several stops to the Chamblee station. We got into my truck and drove to the nearest Waffle House that I could find, over on Peachtree Industrial Boulevard. We went in and sat on the same side of the booth. She lay up against me and groaned.

"You promised to shoot me."

"I have instead decided to revive you."

I ordered a double order of hash browns with ham, cheese, chili, and jalapeños for us to share. I also got two sausage patties, and a double order of wheat toast. "Coffee or soda?"

"Diet Coke, please."

I put my arm around her as she laid her head on my chest. "Can I sleep now?"

"Soon. First, we eat." She groaned again.

She laid her arms on the table and put her head down. I rubbed her back.

The waitress, who was a middle-aged very black lady, came by with the drinks and looked at Kim with some concern. "She okay?"

I said, "We were up late last night."

"Uh-huh. I bet. And you ordered her the hangover special?"

"Yes, Ma'am."

"If she gets sick, take her outside."

I laughed and said, "Yes Ma'am!" again.

The server looked at her again. "Poor thing."

Our food came promptly. As the server set it down, she said, "Here you go, honey. Get some of this food in you, you'll feel better. Your man got you just the right thing."

Kim raised her head, gave a wan smile, and said, "Thank you, Ma'am. If I die here, will you make sure he gives me a decent burial?"

The server laughed. "You ain't gonna die. It just feels like it right down. You'll feel better soon."

I dug into one of the most fabulous breakfast dishes on the planet and got a few bites into Kim. After a bit, she had a few more bites, then a few more. We took our time, and before long, Kim had eaten a healthy portion and was nibbling on the toast.

I asked, "Feeling better?"

"Yes, much. I would have not thought this greasy mess would settle my stomach."

"It's either this or a Whataburger bacon cheeseburger. A Jack in the Box Jumbo Jack does nicely, too. I used to fly with a crazy ex-Navy guy named Bart at the corporate outfit we both worked for that introduced me to this cure."

"Bart was a wise man," she said solemnly.

We finished our drinks, and she went to the restroom while I settled the bill. The same server asked, "How's she doing?"

"Much better, thanks."

Kim was walking back to join me as I stood paying the bill and smiled at the server. The server looked at her and then me.

"You take good care of this sweet girl, you hear?"

"I intend to. Bye!"

We got back in the truck, and Kim asked. "What's next?"

"I've got all the clothes and stuff I need on the boat; we'll stop at a grocery store when we get close and get some supplies."

"Cool. How long is the drive?"

"From here, 45 minutes to an hour maybe."

"If you don't mind, I'm going to curl up and rack out."

I nodded. "I thought you might. There's a little lightweight blanket behind the seat in the extended cab part. You can lean your seat back, too."

She reached around and found the blanket. "Ah! Perfect!"

Curled up into the corner with the blanket over her, Kim was soon asleep. I looked over at her several times. I love the way sleeping women look, with their eyelashes on their cheeks. With no makeup on, she was naturally pretty. I tried my best to drive smoothly, and she got a good restorative nap on the drive to the lake.

After about 45 minutes, she roused as I turned off Interstate 985 at Friendship Road and came to a stop at the traffic light.

"I am pleased to announce that I am back among the living," She said sleepily.

"You don't know how glad I am to hear that."

I pulled into a Publix supermarket, and we went in. We shopped a little, deciding that we would keep it simple and just do burgers and brats for dinners. After asking about her preferences for sodas, beer, and snacks, we checked out and continued on the short drive to the lake. As we were waiting to check out, she put her arm around my waist and leaned her head on my shoulder. I put my arm around her and kissed her forehead.

"You're very sweet when you are acting like a girlfriend."

"Don't you dare tell my squadron mates. They think I'm this masculine bitch."

"Your secret is safe with me."

We continued on to the marina, and Kim exclaimed as we pulled in. "Wow, I had no idea. Look at all these boats!"

Since it was the middle of the week, I was able to park near my dock. We got out and started down the long ramp, with Kim again admiring all the boats. "Crap, there is a lot of money out here. You hang out with rich dudes."

We walked up to my boat, nestled among others of a similar size. "Here we are."

"Jesus, Dirk! This freaking thing is huge!"

"Yeah, it's a good size for having friends overnight."

We went onto the front deck, and I opened the sliding glass door. "Dang, it's hot. Let me get the air conditioning going." I opened the blinds and turned the A/C to a comfortable setting. I then showed her around, and she kept exclaiming her admiration for the amenities, especially the well-stocked bar under a glass hutch. When we got to the back deck, she was excited about the Sea Doo on a ramp at the back. "Are we gonna ride that?"

"You bet, after I clean the boat up a bit. I haven't been out here in a few weeks, and it gets grimy."

"I'll help with the chores. Wow, this is a real chick magnet! You must have a stream of girls wanting to come to hang out."

"I have to have something like this since I have a small dick and no personality."

"Aww, don't sell yourself short. You have a little personality. What can I do to help?"

"How about you clean the sliding glass doors and maybe vacuum the deck while I power wash the upper deck?"

"You got it, boomer. Just show me where the stuff is."

I got out the cleaning crap and vacuum cleaner for her, then I went up to the upper deck and power washed the flybridge area and deck. It wasn't really bad, but I wanted it to look nice for her. It always takes longer than think it will. I was finishing up and rolling up the hoses when I heard voices at the front of the boat, and Kim laughing. She had a nice laugh.

I walked to the stairs and started down as my dock neighbors Jack and Donna were walking away towards their boat. They saw me and waved. "Hi, Dirk!" they called out and I replied. As I went down the stairs, Kim was finishing up cleaning the sliding glass doors. I could see why they had stopped to chat, or at least why Jack had stopped. Kim had changed into a skimpy bright orange bikini and looked stunning.

"Nice outfit!"

"Thanks, I was getting hot, so I changed."

"I see you met my dock neighbors."

"Yeah, Jack and Donna. They're nice. We're going down to their boat for happy hour. I told them we were going to ride the Sea Doo, have some great sex, and then have a nap. Donna is going to make her famous hot spinach and cream cheese dip."

I had to laugh. "I'm glad you have our day all planned out.

"You're welcome. I can tell you are in need of female leadership."

Still laughing, I said, "Donna spoke to you after seeing you in that outfit?"

Kim laughed as well. "I think I did her a favor. Jack was really checking me out. I bet he got a boner and is down there shagging her right now."

The thought of my retired neighbors in their 70s having houseboat sex was a little too much.

I said, "You're all sweaty, and so am I. I'll put my suit on and let's go ride the Sea Doo."

"I wouldn't have gotten sweaty if you did not have me doing manual labor. Do you treat all the girls like this?"

"Most girls are appreciative of the privilege of coming out here and enjoying my company, and work without complaining, unlike my present guest. Do you want a cool drink first, and we could sit in the shade for a few minutes? Bloody Mary?"

"Oooh! Now you are talking. Yes, please."

A ride on the Sea Doo

I made some simple Bloody Mary's and we sat on the back deck in the shade and watched the lake for a while. She started asking about the Sea Doo and how it worked, so as we sipped our drinks, I showed her the controls and the features. She wanted to look in the engine compartment and crawled out on the water port to look at the jet pump exhaust, the reversing mechanism, and the reboarding step.

She finished her drink. "Okay, drink up, let's go! Time's a wasting!"

I had a few more swallows left. "Has anyone told you that you are an overbearing pain in the ass?"

"Yeah, I get that all the time. Where are the life jackets?"

I got the life jackets, and we spread some sunscreen on our faces and necks. I untied the Sea Doo and pushed it off, and she climbed on the back. It started right up, and we idled out of the no-wake zone towards the main lake. There wasn't anyone on the lake, that's another reason I like coming out during the week.

"I've just got my arms around you to hang on, don't get any ideas," she said.

"Funny you should mention that. I have a few ideas." She responded by stroking my leg, which felt nice.

We rode around for a while, just cruising. After a while, she said into my ear, "Can I drive?" I had wondered how long it would be before she asked me.

"Sure thing." I idled down and shut it off. "Let's stop it and get in the water and do a reboarding drill first."

"Good idea." We had similar backgrounds and believed in practicing emergency and abnormal procedures. She slid off the back into the water, and I followed, holding on to a short rope.

"This is in case the wind blows the thing away from us."

"Another good idea. Come here."

I swam the short distance to her, where she put her arms around my neck, pulled me in, and kissed me for a nice interval. "Thanks! What was that for?"

"I just felt mushy for a minute. I'll get over it. Let's go!"

We performed the pain-in-the-ass reboarding drill, kneeling on that stupid little bar and pulling ourselves up onto the jet ski. She did it effortlessly, which made me envious. I always had to strain to get up. She was on the seat already, getting ready to go. I slid up behind her, she asked for a minor clarification on the controls, then started it and we began idling in forward thrust as she played with the steering to figure out low-speed maneuvering.

I was just telling her to ease in the throttle to get us on plane when she increased the power a little bit and then nailed full power. I slid back on the seat, with my wet trunks having minimal traction on the vinyl seat. I thought I was going overboard and grabbed her around the waist. She accelerated to near maximum speed, let out a "Woooo!" and started some turns left and right to get the feel. Her ponytail was whipping me in the face, so I tucked it into her life jacket. Soon she was putting us into sharper and sharper turns, exploring the limits. She was turning hard back and forth, going back over our wake, getting some air as we smashed through. Damned fighter pilots.

I yelled over the wind and engine noise, "If you crash this thing you are paying for it!" The response was mad laughter. I hung on grimly. After several minutes, she slowed back to idle and said, "That's fun! I'm getting kind of randy. You can play with my boobs under the life jacket if you want."

"Who says randy anymore, are you a Brit?" as I tried to slide my hands up under her life jacket. "That doesn't work very well."

"Well, damn, boomer! Loosen up the straps. Must I do everything?" She loosened up the straps a little, and I tried again. "Yeah, I see. Not all that satisfactory. Okay, you can slide your hand in my swimsuit bottom then." I did, and she must have thought that was satisfactory, as she hit the gas and took off again, with me playing with what I could reach in her shorts. It was pretty fun.

After some rapid maneuvering, she slowed down and asked, "Is there anywhere we can just swim?"

"Yeah, either in the middle of the lake or there are some small beaches over there." I pointed. She aimed the Sea Doo in the direction of the beaches. When we got close to shore, she idled down, and I told her to kill the engine about 10 feet from shore so we did not suck sand into the impeller. She did, and the nose of the jet ski slid smoothly up onto the sand. We jumped off into the water, and I pushed the ski a little farther up the beach so it would stay put.

She said, "Ah, that feels good after being hot." We took off our life jackets and tossed them up on the Sea Doo so they would not get sandy and just floated around for a couple of minutes, then she swam over to me. "Can you stand up here?"

"Yep. So should you, you're as tall as I am." We were in chest-deep water. She put her arms around me and kissed me. I put my arms around her, too. I thoroughly enjoyed that and found out that holding a tall, attractive, nearly naked woman in a close embrace after a thrilling near-death experience on a jet ski while kissing was kind of stimulating. My cock woke up and was trying to get out of my suit. She broke the embrace and stripped off her top and bottoms, tossing them onto the jet ski.

"Your turn! Skinny dipping is in progress!"

I looked around. We had the lake to ourselves. Unless someone was hiding in the vegetation on shore, we were hidden. I pulled off my trunks and added them to the pile on the Sea Doo. We embraced again, and I kissed her. After a minute, she pulled back and said, "Boomer! You have a nice boner! A boomer boner!" She giggled.

"Yes indeed, you have that effect on me. Let's get back to the boat and do something about that."

"Ah, I disagree. There's no time like the present!" And with that, she raised up a little as she grabbed my cock and slid it into her pussy. "Oh yeah! I've been wanting to do that ever since I pushed my boobs into you on the airplane a few weeks ago. Remember?"

"How could I forget? But you wanted me to fuck you in a lake way back then?"

"No, dumbass! Just the part about... oh never mind. Are you just going to stand there?"

"Nope!" I started a rhythmic thrusting into her, and she wrapped her long legs around me, increasing the pleasure immensely. She pushed into me as best she could, using her legs to pull me in at the appropriate point of each thrust. It was quite stimulating.

We kissed deeply, and I realized I was holding her up by the ass cheeks. I freed a hand and found her tits and started fondling her and tweaking her long nipples. She made a long moan of appreciation, and we frothed the water for several minutes until I could take no more and loosed a load of cum into her cunt, mixed with lake water. I groaned as I came, with a few additional jets of cum spurting forth. I slowed down, then stopped, out of breath as I held her up. I said, "Damn! That was nice."

"You're welcome. It was a first for me. Maybe not the last, it was very refreshing." We broke the embrace as my cock quickly shriveled in the cool water. After another kiss, we paddled around in the water for a few minutes. She said, "This lake sex is okay! Makes clean up a breeze."

"I had not thought of that. Very efficient. Ready to head back in?"

"Yep. You should probably drive, I have no idea where I am going and I am not ready to try and dock yet."

I put my trunks on, donned my life jacket, pushed the Sea Doo off the beach, and turned it around. I noticed that Kim had started to put her jacket on, then remembered that she was naked. "That vinyl did not feel great on my nipples." She did look pretty great naked on the beach.

I climbed on the Sea Doo, as she pushed us off the beach a little, then mounted up. "Ready, Sir!" I hit the starter and we eased around to an approximate heading back to the marina, eased the gas on, and smoothly accelerated to a reasonable cruise speed. I yelled back to her, "That's the approved airline style of operation."

Her reply was, "You drive like an old man!"

A great episode back at the boat

On arrival back at the boat, we got the Sea Doo pulled up on its custom ramp, shed our life jackets on the back deck, and went directly into the master stateroom through the sliding glass door. We each went to a bathroom, me to the master and her to the guest. I had left my swimsuit in the bathroom and was using a big beach towel to wipe down any residual lake water when she reappeared in the nude, also with a beach towel in her hand, which she spread out on the bed. "I have a request," she stated calmly.

"Go ahead with your request," was my reply like air traffic control would say.

"I request a good shagging! The sex on the beach was fun, and a good start, but I am really horny. Can you do me, please?"

I loved the spontaneity of this girl. "I'll do my best, considering it was about a half hour ago that we did standup lake sex."

"In that case, you can show me what you have for oral skills." She climbed up on the towel spread out on the master bed, turned toward me, and spread her long, pretty legs.

I went to her, bent down from standing at the foot of the bed, and gave a few exploratory licks on her labia. The lake water bath we had cleaned up most of the sweat and associated stickiness from our chores earlier. She made an approving sound, so I went a little deeper. More approving sounds. Then I noticed we were close to the edge of the towel. I wanted to make the work area safe from spills and drips, so I pulled back.

"Kim, raise up a minute. Let me get this designer bedspread off so we don't stain it."

She had an impatient response. "For Christ's sake, boomer! Do it fast! I'm about to explode here!"

She hopped off the bed, and I gathered the spread in my arms and hurried to the upper guest room, and kind of flung it up onto the bed there without folding it, hurrying back to the master bed. Kim had already arranged the towel back on the bed, assumed the position, and was fingering herself with a blissful expression on her face.

"Need a hand?" I asked very wittily.

"Smart ass. That was the longest 30 seconds ever. Yes, you may take over." She pulled her finger out and looked around. I got the idea, reached past her to the bedside table, and pulled out a washcloth. "Wow," she said. "What the hell else do you have next to the bed?"

I slid my middle finger into her pussy. "Oh, the usual. Washcloths, lube, handcuffs, whips."

"Cool. While you were away, I came up with a plan. You will lie on the bed with me and we will sixty-nine each other. When I achieve the desired orgasm, which with what you are doing will be pretty quick – don't stop! – you may mount me and have your way with me. In the event you come before me, you may come in my mouth, and we'll just have to deal with it. Are there any questions?"

"I love a girl that plans and briefs a military operation plan in the bedroom while I am fingering her pussy. I'm in and have no questions."

"Okay, standby to execute ... execute!"

We smoothly lay down together and took positions, placing our heads at each other's crotch. But there was one more detail. She said, "Oops. Do you like the bottom or top?"

"I'll take the bottom, please. That lets you have the freedom to move your head, and I'm sure my balls hanging in your face is not aesthetically pleasing."

She indicated assent. "Good choice, but who says I am going to move my head?"

Her leg swung over my head and I was looking at her pussy from below. I needed her back a little further and tugged on her hips in the desired direction. She understood the request and scooted towards me, and I soon had a face full of pussy. I buried my face in it, reveling in the moment. I moved her legs back a little so that her entire weight was on me. I had a lot of firm, tall, wiggly girl on top of me, and loved it. I don't ever recall having sex with a woman this tall, let alone doing the sixty-nine.

I love eating pussy. The sights, the smell, the textures ... ahhh. Her cunt had the distinct, sharp, anchovy-like aroma that I loved. I had my nose perilously close to her asshole, which was a necessary evil. She had a modest amount of brown pubic hair, which I could feel on my lips.

We both went to work. I started a tour of her pussy south to north and back again with north being the end with the clit. I gave it a tickle each time I went north. On the southbound trip, I stuck the end of my tongue into her vaginal vault. She was squirming and making some great moans as I went about my duties.

She was busy, too. My flaccid dick was waking up due to her attentions, with her tongue circling the shaft and glans. Her head bobbed up and down, increasing the stroke as my dick responded and began getting larger. The moans were somewhat muffled by the dick in her mouth.

In a few short minutes, her squirming and moaning increased to a crescendo and she let loose a long sigh of contentment. "Aaaahhhhh!" and stopped the motion on my dick for a while as she put her head down on my leg as the waves of orgasm swept her. Her hand reached up and pumped my dick while her head was down. After a minute, she announced, "Phase one is complete! You may now mount me."

She rolled off me and squirmed onto her back onto the towel, which was now rumpled. I knelt between her legs, slid my hips up, and moved into her slowly as her hand guided the head of my cock into her waiting pussy. I pushed in with slow strokes, slowly moving deeper and deeper until I had my shaft fully buried in her.

She exclaimed as I reached the bottom of her pussy. "Oh, that's what I have been wanting since I first laid eyes on you. C'mon boomer! Start pushing!"

I complied, and began a rhythmic thrusting into her, as her hips moved against me on each stroke. So many women just lay there, this was incredible. She looked up at me and laughed. "Your face is a mess!" and grabbed the washcloth and gave me a wipe, somewhat complicated by my thrusting motion.

She then wrapped her long legs around my back and pulled me in as I thrust. It was an incredible feeling. I reached up as I held my weight on one arm and fondled her tits, especially enjoying her long nipples and large, dark areola. She managed another moan and moved her hands to my ass to help pull me in.

She then asked, "Are you going to be able to come like this?"

"Probably after a while."

"Let me roll over and you can do me from behind. I have an idea that you will like that."

"Yes, please! Doggie style is my favorite!" I reluctantly pulled out of her, and she scrambled around onto her hands on knees, and again guided my now rock-hard shaft into her dripping wet pussy. I eased into her smoothly, again reaching bottom, drawing a low, "Mmmmmm" from her. I enjoyed the moment, savoring the view of her smooth, tanned back with a thin line where her swimsuit top rested. She had two small dimples at the base of her spine, and had some light hairs along her backbone. My eyes moved down to her ass, which had a nice shape and looked especially inviting with my pubic hair up against it.

"You have a great ass!"

"Thanks! Now quit sightseeing and get to work!"

I took the hint and resumed thrusting. The feeling of being in her vagina at this angle was fantastic. I involuntarily ramped up my rate of movement and pushed hard and deep on every push. She pushed back into me with each thrust, keeping up with my pace.

After a few minutes, the pressure in my balls started to increase, and I began a frenzied attack on her from behind, hearing the sound of flesh slapping against flesh, one of the hottest, sexiest sounds in the world. I could feel the pressure welling up in my cock and was soon spewing hot cum into her in large spurts. I rammed into her and held it as my dick sprayed her insides with several jets of hot juice, and I groaned loudly.

"Damn, Kim! That was nice. Thanks!"

"You are quite welcome. Now snuggle me a little."

I pulled out, my rapidly shrinking dick making a wet plop as it came out of her sopping pussy. I rolled onto my back, and she handed me the washcloth. I wiped some goo off my dick and handed it back to her, whereupon she put it between her legs up against her pussy to keep the juices under control until she could get to the bathroom. She snuggled up to me, putting her head on my chest, and threw a leg over mine. It was very nice.

She said, "Well, boomer. I'd say we are sexually compatible. The first official sex act in the logbook."

"But that's the third time I've come with you in like 24 hours."

"Drunken blow jobs and standup lake sex don't count."

"I see. So, we have had sex once."

"Yes, officially." She ran her fingers through my modest chest hair, as I stroked her ass and back with my free hand. "We must be compatible, to be snuggling even though we are sweaty, have juice all over us, and have been in the lake. After the mandatory snuggling period is up, we shall take a shower and prepare for our social engagement with Jack and Donna."

"Mandatory snuggling? Shower together? Are you planning again?"

"Obviously."

After a brief companionable silence, she shocked me by saying, "You eat pussy pretty well for a man."

"For a man? Uhhh ..."

"Yeah, women are better at oral sex," she said matter-of-factly.

"And you know this how?"

"First-hand experience, my friend!"

"So, you have sex with women, too?"

"Sure. I'm probably bisexual, although I don't like labels. I mostly have sex with men, but I like it with women, too."

I was processing that when she craned her neck and kissed me. "Okay, time to shower!"

"So, the mandatory snuggling period is complete?"

"Again, obviously. Which shower shall we use?" She was on her feet, looking into the master bath. "Hmm. That shower in the bathtub is too small. We'll use the guest bath stall shower. Hit the head and report to the shower after you hear my toilet flush."

"I normally don't like bossy women."

"Yes, but I can tell you adore me. See you in a couple of minutes."

"Yes, Ma'am!"

I met her in the shower as instructed and we had a lovely, soapy shower together, after a brief discussion on the shower temperature. Most women like the water hotter than I like. We reached a compromise, which was the temperature she wanted for this shower, and my desired temperature for our next.

"You're burning my skin off!"

"Don't be a wuss, boomer. Wash my back."

She held her hair up, and I washed her back, and neck, throwing in a kiss on the neck for good measure. She turned around and was in my arms. We kissed as the hot water ran over us, with no room between us. I could feel her nipples and tits against my chest. "Mmmm. You're good at showers. Are you getting a boner?"

"I don't see how so soon after you made me have sex."

"I feel something down there. Okay, shower completed. Commence toweling off. You'll have to step out, there's not enough room to dry off."

We dried off and looked at the clock. "What time did you tell Donna we were coming over."

"She said around 1730. We have time for a short nap. Head for the bed."

"Damned bossy women."

"Ah, you love it, and you know it." She tossed the now somewhat soiled beach towel into my washing machine in the small nook across from the closet, we pulled the sheets back, and collapsed into bed. "Roll over, your turn to get snuggled." She lay up against me, put an arm across me, and a minute later a leg came up over me. I could feel her boobs against my back as she wiggled in closely. It felt very nice.

"Please set a clock for 1700, boomer."

I reached over to the bedside table and fumbled with the clock for a minute. "Done!"

She indicated her approval by kissing the back of my neck. Within minutes, we were both asleep.

Happy Hour with J&D

I awoke to the alarm going off, and looked around. I was alone in the bed. I pulled on some underwear and went looking for my nap mate. She was in the guest bath, combing her hair, naked. It was incredibly erotic. She saw me in the mirror. "About time you got up."

I shook my head.

"Now that you are up, you can help me decide what to wear."

"I like that. What are the choices?"

We walked back to the bedroom, and she pulled a few items out of her helmet bag. "Shorts or skirt?'

I looked at the skirt, it was pretty short. "I like the skirt. It would make your ass and legs look fantastic. Do you have any high heels?"

"No, I have sandals, dumb ass. The skirt it is." She slipped it on, and fastened it, turning around so I could see.

"Very nice! Will you be topless or is there a shirt?"

"I do have a nice white tee shirt to go with this. Should I wear underwear?"

"Yes, I think so. And a bra. I don't want Jack to go into cardiac arrest."

"Okay. Give me a few minutes to finish up, then we can go down. Do we take our own drinks, or do they furnish them?"

"Lake protocol is to take your own drinks."

"Cool. What are you taking?"

I thought for a minute. "I think Jim Beam and diet Pepsi."

"Sounds good. Would you please make me one, as well?"

"You got it." I went to the kitchen, selected two large, insulated tumblers, added ice and a generous portion of Mr. Beam's fine bourbon, and topped it off with diet Pepsi.

Kim came out, finishing hooking one of her earrings. She handed me a gold necklace and asked me to connect it for her. I stood behind her as she lifted her shoulder-length hair and clasped it. I finished with my arms around her waist from behind and kissed her on the ear. "Nice touch, boomer!"

She turned around while I still had my arms around her and kissed me. I admired her. She was tall and well turned out, with the white top and short navy skirt. With her hair down, earrings, necklace, and long, tanned legs over white sandals, she looked stunning. I told her so, and I thought she blushed a little. "I wanted to look nice for you and your friends. Grab the chips and let's go. It's almost 1730."

"It's a two-minute walk. Let's kiss again."

"Later, sex fiend. Us airline guys need to make an on-time arrival. Besides, I know how older people are, they will have been looking down the dock for us for the past ten minutes."

I handed her one of the drinks, and she sipped it. She pronounced it good, and we stepped back out into the Georgia heat. I was wearing a nice polo shirt and fresh shorts, but it was still hot and humid. We started walking down the dock. She slipped her hand into mine, and I looked at her. "Holding hands is expected, Dirk."

"You didn't call me boomer. Holding hands is nice."

"A momentary period of mushiness."

Sure enough, Jack and Donna were on their front deck, looking our way. I murmured, "You were right!" and I pulled their boat over closer to the dock as we stepped aboard.

We said hi all around, and as expected, Jack and Donna were sipping their nightly one Manhattan. Jack asked, "Can I get you a drink?"

"No, thanks, we brought ours. That dip looks great, Donna!"

She dimpled. "I've had the recipe for a while, it's a favorite of our family. I thought Kim might like it."

Kim tried it and raved over it. Donna's smile grew bigger.

Donna said, "We know Dirk fairly well. Kim, please tell us about yourself."

Kim filled them in at a high level, father a career Marine, living all over the world, she served in the Air Force, working for the same company as Dirk ... then I interrupted.

"Kim is an Air Force officer and pilot. She flew the F-16 fighter jet, and now she flies for my airline as a pilot, like me." I got a look containing daggers from Kim.

Jack and Donna were suitably impressed and tripped over themselves asking questions, including how tall she was, which I was curious about. Six feet tall was the answer. The next question was how old and 32 was the answer. I needed both of those nuggets of information. They were good interrogators. They kept exclaiming about her being a fighter pilot. Kim was very humble, which is unlike most fighter pilots. She was really sweet in answering all their questions, and I felt a little bad for setting her up. A little.

After a while, I steered the conversation to their family, and they settled into the usual description of kids and grandkids. After an hour or so had passed, Kim and I had reached the bottom of our glasses. I said, "We are walking over to the restaurant, would you all like to come?" They declined as I knew they would, saying they had supper waiting.

We all stood up, and Kim hugged them both and thanked them for a nice time. Donna said they were taking their pontoon boat out for a ride tomorrow, would we like to come along? Kim said we did not have any real plans besides riding the jet ski in the afternoon, to look us up in the morning.

We stepped off, and as we were walking away, looked back to wave at them. They were watching us to wave goodbye. I was glad I turned around. I took Kim's hand as we walked.

"Holding hands is expected, Kim." She smiled and did not pull her hand away.

"They are a nice couple. Thanks for setting me up for those questions, asshole!" She grumbled.

I was unapologetic. "Hey, you've done a lot. You deserve recognition."

Walking past my boat, I took our glasses and put them inside, then grabbed my wallet. We continued to the shore, walked a few docks over, and arrived at the restaurant. We took a seat and while we waited for a server, Kim asked what the routine was.

"Drinks are expensive, so I usually get whatever beer is on sale, then get either appetizers or a meal. Then I get another drink when I get back to the boat." She agreed with that philosophy and we both ordered the same domestic beer that was on sale.

We looked over the menu, and jointly deciding we were not all that hungry decided on getting appetizers. After consultation, we got fried mushrooms and jalapeno poppers.

Kim then said, "Dirk, the girls that work here all know you and are obviously curious about me. How should I handle this? Am I just Dirk's latest girl to show up? Should I play it cool, or plant a lip lock on you and grab your dick?"

"The second part would be a first for even this place, which has seen a lot of lake romances. How about gazing into each other's eyes while holding hands?"

"I'm down with that. Low key. Mysterious." She reached for my hand that was resting on the table as the server brought our food. She looked into my eyes and smiled. She had the prettiest green eyes. The server smiled, too. We placed our order.

I said, "I think that had the desired effect. She's probably telling the entire staff about the pretty girl Dirk is holding hands with. You can go back to calling me an asshole now."

Kim laughed and said, "Sorry. That was the fighter pilot's reaction. I'll try and be more girly. Or do you like me more fighter pilot-like?"

I said honestly, "I like you for you, whatever you are acting like. In the last 24 or so hours I have started to know you, I have learned that you are wonderfully crazy, have no filter, say any damn thing you like, are without reservation in the bedroom, are a great karaoke partner, and obviously a skilled pilot. You are damned good-looking, tall, athletic, and have the prettiest green eyes. You're a great package deal, I'm honored and glad to be your friend, and I would not have you change a bit."

She looked at me for a long minute with a slight smile on her face. "Thank you, Dirk." Then she looked down at our food. "We'd better eat before this stuff gets cold. Dig in, boomer!"

After we ate, we argued about who would pay, and of course, she won, saying I was hosting her and she was drinking my booze and burning gas out of my jet ski. I'm sure the girls at the restaurant noted that.

We strolled back to the boat hand in hand, even with no audience. We stopped a few times and looked out at the lake as it got dark, each pointing out some lights or some other sight. Once on board, I got us another drink and we climbed the stairs to the upper deck and got out lounge chairs. The night had morphed into a soft, warm breeze, and it was enjoyable just sitting quietly and watching the stars come out. I was really having a good time and said so. Kim answered, "So am I, Dirk. This is really nice."

We were quiet for a long time, then she leaned over and softly asked, "Is there any dessert?" I could not help but laugh. I was expecting something profound.

"Maybe some pop tarts."

"Oooh, yeah. Can we have one?"

I went after the pastries, and we munched them in silence.

"Dirk?"

"Here."

"Did you get freaked out when I told you I had sex with women?"

"Not so much freaked out as surprised. You can certainly do what you want. I was just wondering why you chose to tell me."

"I think I wanted you to know that part about me while you are getting to know me. You know, in case that would make a difference in how you felt about me."

"Thanks. I want to know everything about you. I'm not going to judge you. There are things about me that you may be surprised about, too."

"That's very open and secure of you."

I tried a lighter tact. "Besides, I could get some pointers from you on oral sex. You know, up my game."

"Now you are teasing me to lighten the mood."

"You are a smart girl."

"I appreciate it but still have serious things to say. Like I don't know why my heart skipped a beat and my knees felt weak when you and I stood in the door of the airplane close together a few weeks ago. I immediately knew that I wanted to have sex with you. I HAD to have sex with you. It was visceral."

I looked at her in the dim light. Her face was serious, so I knew it was no time to be flippant. "I felt a spark, too."

"What the hell caused that?"

"I'm a believer in a sexual chemistry attraction that occurs at a subconscious level. It just happens." I decided not to tell her that I have had a lot of women tell me that, not in those exact words.

She shook her head. "This is the first time it happened to me. What do we do now?"

I thought for a minute. "I'd say we have to be careful not to confuse lust for love. I made that mistake one time, and it hurt badly when I figured it out."

"Ouch! Want to talk about it?"

"I think we will, maybe not right now."

She looked out at the lake. "I think you are right for us to not confuse our feelings right now. I'm really enjoying playing romantic boyfriend and girlfriend. But we're not, are we?"

It was my turn to look at the lake. "We are boyfriend and girlfriend when we are together, that feels right. But what will it be when we are not in a romantic setting, or when we see other people?"

She looked at me again. "I guess that's the 64-dollar question."

"Yeah, it is."

She tried to smile in the darkness. "Okay, that's enough heavy relationship shit for our first real day of being together. What shall we do now?"

I smiled at her and reached over to stroke her cheek with the back of my hand. "We sit in the dark and watch the stars until we get sleepy, like boyfriend and girlfriend that are enjoying just being together."

Her smile became full and genuine. "I'd like that."

We held hands and did not say a word for a half hour or so, just looking at the stars and the lake, then we shuffled downstairs sleepily.

Day Two at the lake - Wednesday

She borrowed a tee shirt to sleep in, which looked incredible on her. We brushed our teeth, I locked up, and we fell into bed. We snuggled a bit, then fell quickly asleep, worn out from the day's activities.

In the pre-dawn twilight, I heard her get up to use the restroom, so I did at the same time. Back in the bed, she curled up into me with her face buried in my neck. I could tell she was awake. I stroked her back and ass gently. After a few minutes, she pushed at my shoulder until I was on my back, then crawled on top of me, still with her face buried in my neck. Not knowing what was going on, I rested one hand on her very cute ass and used the other to gently stroke her hair. She had her entire weight on me, except for her legs which were on either side of mine. It was quite pleasurable to have a load of firm, warm girl on top of me. I waited to see what happened next.

After what seemed like a very long time, she raised up into a sitting position, with her hips directly over mine. She took both hands and stripped off the tee shirt, and lay her bare chest back down against mine. I could feel her boobs and nipples against me. That was very sensual, and although she had done nothing else, I could feel my cock waking up and hoped she did not think it was a demand for sex. I was still not sure what she was doing.

Minutes passed, and it was getting light outside, the edge of the heavy draperies allowing some sunlight to peek through. She roused, and her hips pushed against mine a few times. She then rolled off me to her side and reached down and started tugging on the waistband of my underwear. I helped her ease them off. She put my hand on her panties, and with me helping, slid them off and tossed them over her shoulder.

I looked into her now-open eyes for a sign. She looked directly back at me with those pretty green eyes. Then she rolled over onto her back and pulled me on top of her. Still looking directly into each other's eyes, she reached down and took my now fully erect cock and guided me into her, all the time with our eyes locked on each other. It was one of the most erotic things I have ever experienced.

As I slid into her, she let out a long sigh and closed her eyes. I began a nice, slow rhythmic thrusting and she gently moved her hips into me with the same rhythm. I could feel her wet, tight pussy closed around my dick, and her labia felt fantastic as they slid on the shaft of my cock. Her arms went around me, and I felt one of her hands reach up to stroke my hair. I reached up with a free hand and fondled her boobs, which earned me a hip squirm and a soft moan.

We kept the same slow, sweet rhythm for several minutes when my balls indicated that they needed to come. I increased my rate a little and she moaned softly again as I felt the sudden rise of cum building, then I shot it into her as she made another moan and held me tightly with her arms. I stopped thrusting and waited. I felt a couple of more spasms as the last of my cum splashed into her. She was still stroking my hair. It felt fantastic. She sighed softly, "Oh, Dirk!" and opened her eyes to look up at me. I went to climb off, but she held me tightly, indicating that I was to remain on top of her and inside her. I rested my face against her neck and could feel her heart beating against my chest. We fell asleep in that position.

Sometime later, I roused and found myself alone in bed. While using the restroom, I heard furtive sounds from the galley, and as I went out saw Kim wearing the short skirt from last night and the tee shirt I had loaned her. The shirt was hot pink and had the name of the flight school I used to teach at emblazoned on the front. She had brushed her hair and pulled it back into a ponytail, secured by a scrunchie thing. She looked fabulous, and I had a moment of wonder that a plain, nothing-special guy like me in his mid-40s had a beautiful girl like this in his galley.

"Hi, girlfriend!"

She turned and smiled at me. "Hi, boyfriend!"

I went to her and kissed her on the cheek. "What are you doing?"

"Making coffee."

"I had no idea you had domestic skills."

"I should be offended! I have skills outside the bedroom. Go out on the front deck, I'll bring your coffee. What do you take in it?"

"Some half-n-half." I got it out for her. "Just a couple of glugs of creamer ..."

"You'll get it however I decide to fix it, and like it that way. Now, git!"

I retreated to the safety of the front deck. Jack had stuck the morning paper on my table with a rock on it. He walked up to the marina store every day and got a paper and then shared it with me and others when we were in residence. A very nice gesture. After a few minutes of me reading the headlines about mayhem and violence, Kim came out with two coffee mugs.

"Thank you. You're drinking coffee this morning?"

"Yeah, I need a boost with the day I have been planning. What's the dress code, boomer? Am I properly attired"?

"You look great in that skirt thing. I'd say you are good in anything from a swimsuit to an evening gown. By the way, I'd love to see you in an evening gown."

"Dream on, dude. Okay, I'll put on my suit a little later. Should I wear underwear?"

"Not on my account. Are you wearing such items at present?

"Wouldn't you love to find out? Do you have any inputs before I finalize the schedule?"

"Hmm. A little breakfast, then fish while we see if Jack and Donna invite us out in their boat, then Sea Doo in the afternoon. Happy hour. Dinner."

Kim plans the day

"It's a good thing I am your planning officer. Here is the schedule, considering your input: Coffee, breakfast, fishing, boating with J&D, snack, sex on the Sea Doo, showering, abbreviated happy hour, dinner in town, back for after-dinner drinks, cunnilingus tutorial, then lights out for sleep."

"Sex ON the Sea Doo? What!"

"Of the entire schedule, that's what you are fixating on? Yes, I have a few ideas for sex on the machine. You can think about that during the day." She smiled coyly.

"But ..."

About that time my neighbor Gene came ambling up the dock. "Dirk!" He called out and waved as he approached. He was in his 70s, still working at his construction business, and had an accent from the swamps of Georgia that you could cut with a knife.

"Ah din't know you was here!"

"We got in yesterday afternoon. This is Kim."

He shifted his gaze to Kim and smiled hugely as he took her in. "Hi, Kim! What're you doin' hanging around with this guy?"

Kim said, "Hi Gene. It's part of my work release program. Come on and sit with us."

He swung aboard and plopped down, gazing appreciatively at her, then turned to me. "You shoulda tole me you was at the boat. I didn't bring your drink."

By way of explanation, I turned to Kim and said, "Gene is our resident bartender. He makes the best Bloody Mary's on the lake, if not the state. He usually treats me with one when he is here."

Kim said, "Wow! That is a great reference. What all do you put in them?"

Gene replied, "A little of this, a little of that." He stood up. "C'mon Kim, I'll show you how I make 'em."

After a quick look at me to see if I gave her the wave-off or danger sign, Kim said, "Sure!" got up and followed Gene off the boat. He was harmless but loved pretty women. I went back to reading the paper and sipping my coffee.

A few minutes passed, and I could hear them coming back, Gene carrying two of the concoctions, with Kim holding hers. Gene was talking animatedly, and Kim was laughing. All was well.

Kim was laughing as they sat down at the table. "You ought to see what he puts in these things. Celery, shrimp, a piece of okra, jalapeno olive. Anything I missed, Gene?"

"A slim Jim!"

"And a slim Jim! We had a tasting, then reloaded ours and brought you yours."

The drinks looked awesome. We toasted, clinking the plastic solo cups together, and sat back to savor the drinks.

I said, "Magnificent as always, Gene!" He beamed.

Kim chimed in, "These are the best I have ever had! Thanks so much!"

We chatted for a while, marina gossip mainly, then Gene asked, "Kim, may I ask what you do besides being a professional beauty queen?"

She said, "Aww, you're sweet. I'm an airline pilot, I work for the same company that Dirk does."

Gene grinned and said, "That's cool! I'm gonna have to fly somewhere so you can be my pilot!"

I chimed in. "She's an Air Force veteran, too ..."

Kim gave me a dirty look, and said, "I'm also an Air Force pilot. I flew F-16s and am now in the Air National Guard still flying them."

Poor Gene almost lost it. "That's freaking incredible! Beautiful and lethal! What a package. Would you consider marrying an old redneck like me?"

She laughed, got up and kissed his cheek, then sat back down. "That's a great offer, but I'm not ready to get married for a while."

He was flustered for a while as we finished our drinks. After a few minutes of chit-chat, he got up and said, "Well, I gotta go back to work. I just came out to check on my boat, and I'm real glad I did! Bye!"

We stood up and waved to him as he ambled off and thanked him again for the drinks.

I said, "You made Gene's day! He's got a story to tell his guys at work."

"He's sweet. You have nice friends, Dirk. But going back to work at 9 something in the morning after a drink ..."

I just shrugged. We went in and each had a toaster waffle and sausage patty. I put peanut butter and syrup on my waffle, which she thought was bizarre.

We both cleaned up the minimal mess and rinsed our coffee mugs. She looked around, said, "I do believe fishing is next. I'm going to change into my suit first."

"Okay, I'll go around to the back deck and get the gear." I was almost out the front door when she called out to me from the master bedroom down the hall.

"Hey boomer!" She had pulled the tee shirt off, revealing that she did not have a bra on. Then she grinned as she lifted the hem of the skirt, which confirmed that she was not wearing underwear. Poor Gene. I hope he did not notice, or he would be headed to the emergency room with a smile on his face.

By the time I had a couple of light fishing rods out at the front of the boat, she was on the front deck wearing a different bright-colored, skimpy bikini that looked great on her. She was pulling on a tank top of a contrasting color that showed her broad, athletic shoulders. Stunning.

I asked, "Do you want a hat or visor to keep the sun out of your eyes?" She did, and we went back inside. I showed her a drawer under the upper guest room bed where I stored various items left by previous visitors, many of them female. In honor of the fictional character Travis McGee by author John D. McDonald, I called it the broad bin as Travis did onboard his houseboat. Among the items were caps and visors. She rooted around the bin and came up with a nearly new visor.

Then she saw something and reached in to pull out a negligee of beautiful diaphanous material, nearly see-through. She looked at me with a smile and a raised eyebrow. "Really, boomer? Someone just forgot this?"

In my defense, I said, "Hey, I have married couples and single friends come out here. It could have been left by anyone."

We walked hand in hand down the dock, each holding a fishing pole in an unoccupied hand. "There's a shady spot under a shelter up by the gate, we'll try our luck there." I got her set up with a light rod with some little bait pellets. "Just let the bait down about a foot under the water. If there are bluegill or perch here, they will attack that in no time."

"Okay, what do we do with them?"

"Just toss them back unless they are gut hooked, then I keep them for cut bait for catfishing."

"We're not going to eat them?" She asked.

"No, I don't like to eat fish."

She shook her head. "You like to fish but don't like to eat them. You're an interesting man, boomer."

Within a minute, a fish had grabbed her bait and was trying to run off. She gave a squeal of delight, pulled in the fish, and admired him for a moment. "You're a pretty little guy!" Then she expertly took ahold of the fish and removed the hook, looked at him up close, kissed him on top of the head, and tossed him back into the water. She wasn't squeamish at all about handling the fish.

"Lips that kiss fish will not touch mine."

"Ah hell, boomer. I'll disprove that in about 30 seconds. Besides, it wasn't a deep kiss."

"You are pretty comfortable handling fish," I said admiringly.

"Yeah, my Dad and I have been fishing a lot. He refused to treat me like a girl and made me do everything."

"Good for Dad. I'd like to meet him someday."

She gave me a look. "I think we are a little early in this relationship to start meeting parents."

"Hell, do we even have a relationship? I'm confused."

"Yeah, me too." She went back to fishing, catching, and releasing a few more.

I noticed that I was watching her and not fishing. "Kim?"

She looked up. I said, "This morning was nice."

Her face lit up. She looked angelic. "Yes, it was. I woke up feeling a little vulnerable, so I just wanted to lay on you for comfort. Then, one thing led to another. It was different, making love instead of fucking like rabbits."

"It's a phase."

"Making love or fucking like rabbits?"

"The second thing. It's the 'fuck each other's brains out' phase where no serious decisions can be made."

She nodded. "Agreed."

We wrapped up the fishing and headed back to the boat. Jack was walking our way as we got to the houseboat. "You kids want to go with us on the pontoon boat? Donna wants to go in a few minutes before it gets hot."

We indicated that would be great, dropped off our fishing stuff, and grabbed our life jackets and bottles of water, following him down the dock to where they kept a nice pontoon boat. Donna was already on board in her favorite seat. We called out hello to Donna as we approached.

"Hi, Dirk! Hi, Kim! So glad you could join us."

We helped Jack loosen the lines, and after he got the engine running, I turned the last line loose and climbed aboard, while Kim was chatting with Donna. I'm a believer in not untying all the lines until the boat is running, I've seen too many boats drift away from the dock while the owner is grinding away on the starter.

They wanted to know all about what we had been doing, so Kim filled them in on going to the restaurant, having a nightcap under the stars, having drinks with Gene, and fishing. Donna had a few comments as she chuckled. "That Gene! What a character. I'm sure you made his day by helping him make drinks. And having a drink while watching the stars! How romantic!" Kim just looked at me and smiled. I smiled back. It was a moment. Then Jack chimed in, "Great, Dirk! Now Donna is going to want to do that instead of letting me watch my TV shows!" Donna ignored him, as I am sure she had been doing for many years.

We cruised around the lake for a while, with Jack pointing out various sights at the different marinas and other points of interest. Then he asked, "Do you kids want to ride the tube? We got it for our grandkids, they really like it." I had noticed a large inflatable thing on the stern, it was a variety that the riders could sit up on. I thought that was a hell of a lot better on the back than lying on your stomach. Miss Kim was of course up for anything fun. "Sure!" she chirped.

Jack slowed the boat to a stop, and I heaved the inflatable off the stern after making sure the tow rope was connected at both ends. Kim was standing up and had reached for the hem of her tank top when she hesitated. Donna picked up on that right away. "You can take your tank top off to get in the water, dear. If Jack's eyes bug out, I'll put them back in for him." He looked chagrined, and I had to look away to keep from laughing. Kim managed the situation by taking off the tank top and putting on the life jacket while facing away from Jack. He may have been disappointed.

We managed to board the inflatable with some semblance of dignity. I called out, "Take it easy on us, Jack! If we get hurt, we can't work on Saturday." Donna assured us that she would keep Jack in check. We drifted to the end of the rope, then Jack accelerated, and we were soon bouncing along, with Kim exclaiming happily as he turned back and forth sharply, and we bounced in the air over the wake. Kim had a question.

"When are you taking me home?"

I thought about it as we bounced along. "This is Wednesday, I think. We both are on four days off that started on Tuesday. So, Tuesday, Wednesday, Thursday, and Friday. We have to be back no later than Friday afternoon for work on Saturday. You have reserve duty and I have a trip. When do you want to go?"

She looked at me with a grin, ponytail flapping in the breeze, sunglasses on, floppy visor, drops of water on her face from the splashing, bouncing along on the tube. She looked incredibly outdoorsy and sexy. "I don't ever want to go home!"

My heart skipped a beat as I looked at her and smiled.

Jack drug us around for a while, then slowed to a stop. We said we had fun and thanked him. He pointed to a nearby sandy-looking beach. "I'll pull over there to the beach. Donna wants to get in the water for a bit. Just stay in the tube." We gave him a thumbs up and he slowly motored us over to the beach.

Kim looked at me as we bobbed along. "Is that the beach we pulled the Sea Doo up yesterday?" She looked mischievous.

"It may be. I've lost track of all the beaches I've had stand-up water sex on." She punched me in the shoulder.

"Owww! Is that any way to treat your host?"

"You deserve it. Anyway, we may need to find a similar beach for this afternoon."

We were still well out of earshot of the pontoon boat.

"Yeah, tell me about your plan for Sea Doo sex."

"Wouldn't you like to know? You'll find out later. Anticipation makes the weenie harder."

I had to laugh. We were definitely in that phase.

Beaching the pontoon boat, we pulled ourselves in with the tow rope, and both Jack and Donna got in the water. We paddled around for a while, chatting. I was glad I did not have to get out of the water right then, thinking about the upcoming Sea Doo events was having a visible effect on me.

We climbed out after a bit and sat dripping. I had forgotten towels. Jack backed the boat out, then asked Kim if she would like to drive us back to the marina. Her eyes lit up, and she happily jumped into the control seat, and with Jack leaning over her and getting an eyeful, she started to drive us. I called out to Donna, "Hang on! She's a crazy fighter pilot!" Donna had a look of concern. Kim resisted the urge to give me the finger and just said she would drive sedately.

Arriving back at the marina safely, we helped tie up the boat and declined an offer of lunch. Kim said, "Dirk is wanting to ride the Sea Doo. We'll see you guys later." I looked at her out of the corner of my eye. My wanting to ride both her and the Sea Doo was at the forefront of my thoughts. We went back to the houseboat and sat on the forward deck as we were still a bit wet. Kim went into the galley and came back with a granola bar and water for each of us.

I said, "What the hell? This is lunch?"

Kim smiled sweetly. "You need to watch your waistline."

That was true, but this ... I sighed. "Damned bossy women."

"Ah, quit complaining. Okay, since we are simulating boyfriend and girlfriend, we have to get to know each other. Time for Q&A."

I could not imagine what this would entail. "Shoot!"

Kim said, "I'll get us started. Puppies or kittens?"

"Both."

"Agreed. Favorite dog breed?"

"Labrador."

"Good choice. Boxers or briefs?"

"Briefs, definitely. They made us wear boxers in basic training."

"So, I have observed. Aren't you worried about sperm motility by wearing briefs?"

"I am doing my best to not father any children, so that answer is no. By the way, are you using some form of birth control?"

Kim looked thoughtful. "I suppose I should since you insist on pumping semen into me at every opportunity."

She looked at me and laughed. I suppose my face had given me away. "Got you on that one, boomer. Don't worry, that situation is covered."

"Thank you very much."

"Do you play golf?"

"Nope. You?"

"Yes, occasionally with my Dad or some friends. You can come with me when I practice by myself, drive the cart, hand me beers, and tell me how cute I look in my little golf skirt."

"I can do that. I can also try and putt."

"Okay, we can go golfing. What other activity can we do away from the bedroom? How about guns? Do you like to shoot pistols?"

"Haven't done it except for small arms qualification in the Air Force."

"That's a yes, you will like that." She paused. "How about sporting clays?"

"What's that?"

"Shotguns and clay targets. You'll like that, too."

"I tried to shoot skeet once, couldn't hit crap."

"There's a lot of technique, I'll show you. Your turn. What do you like to do?"

"I like some quiet stuff like reading."

"Hmm. What authors do you like?"

"I like some military stories by this guy called WEB Griffin. Cool series on Army guys, and another on Marines. I also like pulp fiction novels by John D. MacDonald."

"Okay, I'll try those. Do you envision this as a group activity, you and I reading together? Sounds like something for old folks."

"It's very intimate, a nice evening activity away from the damned TV."

"Yeah, I can see that. What else?"

"I like to walk around the cities I layover in."

"Walking, that's nice. How about hiking?"

"As long as it's not too hilly."

"Wuss. Okay, I'm dry. Want to go for a ride?" She grinned.

"I'm ready!"

She laughed. "You about jumped out of the chair!"

"Ah, hell. We should get gas on the way out of the marina."

Fun on the water

We put on our life jackets again and went to the back of the houseboat to launch the jet ski. "I'll drive over to the gas dock, then you can drive out on the lake if you want."

"Oh, goody! Yes please."

We idled over to the gas dock, with Kim occasionally stroking my legs that she was straddling.

"Stop that, I might crash into the dock while you are distracting me."

"Think of this as channeling your attention, like that scene in 'Fate is the Hunter.'"

"You read that book? I'm impressed."

"Of course. Look out for the dock, you're going to hit ..."

I saved the docking maneuver at the last second and was greeted by a teenage boy and girl. "Hi Dirk!"

"Hi guys, just gas today, please. Say hi to my friend Kim."

"Yessir. Hi, Kim!" The boy held us against the dock, while the girl got the fuel hose.

After a few minutes, our fuel supply was replenished, and with Kim driving, we cranked up and headed for the lake. She commented, "I bet they are already spreading the word about the tall chick Dirk had on his jet ski this time."

"I hope so, it would increase my reputation immeasurably."

"I want to help with the gas, how does that work? Do they bill you?"

"They just use a credit card I have on file, don't worry about it."

"I am worrying about it; I don't want to be a mooch. I'll buy dinner."

"That's fine with me. Okay, here is the end of the no-wake zone, you can accelerate. Gently!"

She hammered the throttle, and the Sea Doo took off like a dragster. I was ready and hung on for dear life as she laughed delightedly. I grumbled about fighter pilots and put my arms around her. It was very pleasant, except when she was terrifying me. I yelled in her ear, above the wind noise. "I believe you mentioned sex on a Sea Doo?"

I could hear her laughing again.

"Down, boy! Besides, I have to get worked up first!"

"I'm already worked up!"

She laughed again, "I know, I feel your boner in my back!"

We rode around for a while, with her doing hard turns and circling back on our wake to jump over it. I was beginning to think I should have stayed on the beach. We had traveled a considerable distance when she slowed and turned in towards a cove. "How's this?"

"It is pretty far from any of the marinas, and being a weekday, there are very few boats. It's about as secluded as it gets."

She pulled into the cove and ran us up on the beach, shutting the engine off well away from the shore as I had shown her yesterday. "Hey, you're trainable!"

"Shut up. Stand by for the briefing. The briefing follows: We will dismount at the beach and remove our swimsuit bottoms, stowing them in the jet ski. You will then lay on your back on the seat, whilst I perform fellatio on you for a brief period. Remember, fellatio is an officer word for a blow job."

"Got it!"

"Don't interrupt the briefing officer. We will then trade positions, with me laying on my back on the seat, at which point you will perform a brief cunnilingus episode until I announce the progression to the next action item. With me so far?"

"Yes, Ma'am. Cunnilingus is an officer word for pussy licking."

"Exactly! Very good. Upon direction, you will cease cunnilingus and mount me while I lay upon the seat. The time period for this is TBD."

"Got it. What's after that?"

"Sir, that is classified. I'll get to that at the appropriate time. Commence operation!"

She was certifiable. I hopped off onto the sand, pulled off my trunks, and handed them to her, as she had her bottoms off already. With the bottoms stowed safely, I lay on my back on the seat, which was not all that comfortable. Standing in the footwells of the ski facing me, she bent down and took my very hard dick into her mouth and started a nice blow job, working her tongue around the shaft and glans. It felt wonderful.

After a short period, she raised up, announced, "Shift position!" and stepped off the ski onto the beach. I hopped down as best I could with a raging hard-on, then go back on the ski facing her as she lay on the seat on her back, spreading her legs a bit. I bent down carefully since the Sea Doo was half in the water and was pretty unstable. I put my face down into her magnificent muff and went to work.

As I gave her delightful pussy some attention, a loud moan escaped her mouth. I was doing the best I could under the circumstances and appreciated any commentary. I went up and down the lips a few times, gave the clit a few gentle licks, and stuck my tongue down into the vaginal vault a few times. From the noises I heard, I was doing a good job. She then gasped out, "You may mount me, sir!"

I raised up, wiped my mouth with the back of my hand, and moved forward on the seat. My meat missile was aimed at the gateway, and she guided it between the lips. As I eased all the way into her hot cunt, a ragged moan escaped her lips. I pumped for a few short strokes and started getting serious with deeper, harder thrusts. Her hips raised up to meet mine at every thrust.

I took a moment to appreciate the situation. I was fucking my friend on a jet ski in broad daylight, out on a lake with the sun beating down on my life jacket – we both still had the jackets on, I was not sure why at that point – we both had our sunglasses on, we were half naked, with sandy feet, humping away as the Sea Doo was bobbing on the water, perilously close to becoming unbeached. It was awesome.

Then she said, "Boomer! Don't come yet, there's more!"

I was astounded. "What!"

She said, "Dismount, we're going to switch."

I reluctantly backed out and stood by.

"Okay, you get on the seat facing backward up at the front. I'll straddle you facing forwards."

That sounded interesting. We wiggled around and traded positions, how we did that without turning the Sea Doo over, I had no idea. I slid my naked butt as far forward as I could, facing aft. She had pushed us off the beach and climbed on while I was doing that. She then swung aboard, and with her straddling me, carefully guided my pole into her pussy. She hit bottom and grinned at me. "This is fun!" She then proceeded to rock back and forth, grinding her pelvis against mine, sliding up and down my dick at the same time. It was very, very sensuous. It reminded me of a time on a horse a long time ago ... never mind.

She had more. "Okay. New rules! Whoever comes first buys the drinks tonight!"

"You're on!" This was a no-lose scenario, and it added an element of fun to an already very sexy situation.

"No cheating! You gotta call it!"

"Yeah, I'm in!"

Then she did it.

She hit the starter, and the Sea Doo came to life.

"What the hell!" I yelled. Her response was to hit the throttle. The Sea Doo raised up out of the water, getting on plane in a few seconds as we slid towards the aft edge of the seat and the water. Between us, we managed to stay aboard. She was laughing as she kept humping me, and then started doing some turns, harder and harder as she kept up the speed of the jet ski and her hips. This was so crazy it was unbelievable! Then she circled back to go over our wake. The impact of the ski going over the wave drove me into her like a pile driver. "Oh, shit! That was wild!"

She humped me ever faster and cranked the Sea Doo around for another pass. I could not hear moaning, but she was biting her lip. Wham! The ski hit the other wake, and she cried out, "Oh. My. God!" and pulled us around again. I had a brief moment of panic and hoped she was looking out for other boats or the shore. I was trying to watch what was going on, keep up my humping, all while fearing for my life and hers. It was kind of intense.

Wham! The ski hit another wave, she cried out, and released the throttle all at once. The ski came off plane immediately and slowed to idle. "Aaahhhhhh! Damn! Oh, shit that feels good!" as she continued to try and hump me through the seat. The Sea Doo swung lazily in a circle as nobody was at the controls for the moment. I kept my rate of humping, trying to throw her off the jet ski with my hips, then I came in a torrent, sending wave after wave of hot cum into her while she collapsed on me.

"Damn, boomer! That was cool!"

"You are one crazy-ass fighter and jet ski pilot! Yes, it was very cool. Amazing, in fact."

She raised her head, looked around, then turned the jet ski towards a beach about a hundred yards away, and we idled towards the shore. She moved her face to mine, and we kissed for the first time in the entire operation. She then moved her face to my neck for a moment.

"Kim? Are you watching where we are going?"

"Oh, shit." She raised up and resumed piloting duties. Soon she cut the engine and we slid up on the beach. "Permission to disembark, Sir?"

"Permission granted. Meet me at the stern for a debriefing."

We climbed off, stripping off our life jackets, with Kim pulling her top off and tossing it on the ski. Totally naked, we walked a few feet into the deeper water and sank down into the coolness. "Ahh, that's great! I was getting hot." She said.

We embraced in the cool lake water and kissed again a few times. I could not stand it anymore. "Where did you get that crazy idea?"

"I came up with the concept of phase one yesterday and phase two appeared to me as we were riding over here. I never planned on starting the ski and driving around perched on your dick, but it seemed like the thing to do at the time."

"Going over those waves was amazing!"

"Yeah, that was intense. I may have some bruising, but it's worth it. Hey, who came first?"

"I couldn't tell. Call it a draw?"

"Sure. You can buy the first round, I'll buy the second."

"Deal."

We splashed around for a while, then got out, reclaimed our suits, and put the life jackets back on. I pushed the Sea Doo off the beach, turned it around, and climbed on.

She gave us a push and climbed on after. I started the thing up and headed for the marina at a sedate pace. Her arms were around me and every now and then she would stroke my legs. I could tell her head was laid sideways against my neck. I took my left hand and found hers, and we intertwined our fingers. "Tired?" I asked.

"Yes, but in a good way."

We docked the Sea Doo at the houseboat and stripped off our life jackets, and n went straight into the shower. There, we took a nice, long, soapy, warm time washing each other and rinsing each other off. It was fun and while erotic, we were both too spent from our exertions to start another round. We got out, toweled off, and climbed into bed for an impromptu afternoon nap. Since I was sleeping with the scheduling officer, I assumed it had been penciled into the schedule.

I awoke first and tip-toed into the living room after grabbing a polo shirt, underwear and shorts. After getting dressed, I sat in my recliner chair and turned on the TV news at a very low volume to get the early weather forecast. I wanted to take the houseboat out, but it was so hard to park with any wind that I had to be very judicious in choosing the days for excursions.

After about 15 minutes, Kim came out, yawning and stretching while pulling on the same tank top over very short white shorts that showed off her long, tanned, legs. She came over and plopped down in my lap sideways to me and put her arms around my neck while nuzzling her face into my neck. I put my arms around her and stroked her thigh since that's where my hand ended up. She yawned again.

"Mmmm. That was heavenly. Why did I fight naps when I was a kid? They are the best thing ever."

"That's one of the many things you learn to appreciate when you get older."

After a cozy minute or two, she got up and went over to the fridge. "Want anything to drink?"

"I think just water right now. It's almost happy hour."

She got us both a bottle of water and sat down on the couch, taking a long pull of hers.

Another Happy Hour with J&D

We watched the news for a few minutes, just relaxing. About that time, I heard a knock on the front sliding glass door and saw Donna peering through the tinted glass. I opened the door. "Hi Donna!"

"Hi, Dirk. Hi, Kim. We wanted to invite you for happy hour, I know you have plans for dinner, but come have a drink first. Don't bring your drink, though. Jack has a surprise for you."

We both said we appreciated the offer and would be down soon. Kim got up. "I need to brush my hair and do some girl stuff. Entertain yourself for a few minutes. Try and stay out of the booze."

"Damned bossy fighter pilots, I mean Yes, Ma'am."

A relatively short time later, Kim emerged in a pretty, short-sleeved collared blouse in a bright floral pattern tucked into the white shorts. She had put on a little eye makeup, brushed her hair out to fall on her shoulders, and had earrings and a tennis bracelet on. "Here, can you help me with my necklace?" As I had done yesterday, she lifted her hair as I fastened the necklace. I put my arms around her and appreciated the feel of the tall, firm, pretty girl in my arms. I kissed the side of her neck. "Mmmm. Don't start that, we'll never make it off the boat."

I let her go and she turned towards me. I asked, "How did you get all that stuff in your helmet bag? I thought I watched you pack a few tee shirts and some bikinis?"

She laughed. "I must have had a moment of clarity when I packed. This is about it, I'm down to a tee shirt and one more swimsuit. I guess I was not planning on an extended stay. I may have to wash clothes."

"We can do that. You look very nice."

She turned a pirouette in front like a model, dimpled, and said, "Thank you, sir. You had a nice shirt on, and we were going to town for dinner, besides I wanted to look nice for happy hour with J&D."

"They will, as I do, appreciate it. I say again, you look stunning."

"Stop, you're embarrassing me. Let's go."

We strolled down the dock, hand in hand. Kim asked, "What do you think the surprise is?"

"I truly have no idea."

Stepping onto their boat, we were greeted by Jack and Donna, and he immediately went to his glass hutch counter, which on most houseboats served as the bar. He turned around and proudly held out cocktail glasses, he announced, "Manhattans for all!"

We exclaimed our gratitude, and after we all had a glass, he raised his glass to us. "To wonderful lake friendships!" We clinked glasses and then sat down.

As we sipped our drinks and made appreciative sounds, Jack and I chatted about marina things, his pontoon boat, and other things. Donna leaned over to Kim and said softly, "Papa does not make his famous Manhattans for just anyone. He wanted to make them for you and Dirk because he really likes you both." Kim expressed her thanks and said we really liked them as well. It was a sweet moment.

After a nice visit over cocktails, they said we should be getting on to dinner. We all stood up, Kim hugged them both and thanked Jack for the special drinks. He beamed with pride. As we walked out, Donna mentioned they would be going home for a few days in the morning, so we would be on our own for happy hour. We assured them we would make do, and waved goodbye as we walked back to our boat. Kim told me about what Donna said about Jack making us his special drink. "They are a sweet couple, Dirk. I really like them."

"And they really like you, I can tell."

We stopped by the boat to pick up the truck keys and my wallet, along with her small purse. As we got to the truck, Kim's eyes flashed as she said, "Can I drive?"

"You sure like to drive, don't you? Sure, I don't care."

She got behind the wheel and looked around. "We are pretty close to the same size. I don't even need to move the mirrors."

Dinner in town

I gave her directions, and we headed toward the town of Buford, GA. Her driving was like she flew an F-16, fast and abrupt. After many years of flight instructing, I managed to remain calm, but it was a task.

We decided on a seafood place close by that had a bar, so we could get both drinks and dinner. Settling at a table, I again admired Kim. She looked great, and I was again wondering why a fantastic girl like this was hanging around with a plain guy like me. She looked up at me.

"Why are you looking at me like that?" she asked.

"I'm in amazement that a girl like you is hanging around with a guy like me."

"It's probably the boat, the Sea Doo, and great sex."

"In that case, I'll never sell the boat."

Kim reached across and took my hand about the time the server came to take our drink order. The server smiled. We all smiled. After placing the drink order, we held hands for a minute, then sat back. She said, "We are poster children for young couples in love. Are we in love?"

"Still too soon to tell. This phase involves a lot of raging hormones and loss of blood flow to certain parts of the anatomy."

"I move to table the love discussion until this phase subsides. Question: When will that be?"

"Uncertain at this point. Could be days, weeks, or months. Who knows?"

"I'm still having fun being boyfriend and girlfriend."

"Me, too."

We chatted over drinks and talked about things we had in common or liked. After recalling I was not a real fan of seafood (I like shrimp, though), we had a second drink and then decided to walk next door to a casual Jamaican place. They had some interesting dishes, and in discussing the menu, Kim leaned close to my ear and said, "Don't eat too much. You are still on the schedule for a cunnilingus tutorial following the after-dinner drinks."

"I'm sure we are the only couple in line having that discussion. Want to split a dish? I'm trying to watch how much I eat."

We got the dish and split it at the table, looking I'm sure like a couple comfortable with each other, although adding up the days, this was really the second full day we had spent together. At this rate of activity, I would be worn to a frazzle soon. It was a wonderful problem to have.

I looked around the room at the other couples. Kim noticed. "What are you looking around at?"

"I'm trying to guess how many guys here are going to get a cunnilingus tutorial tonight."

"Only the lucky ones, dude."

We finished up and walked back to the truck. I told Kim, "I'd better drive back. We have both had drinks and are probably okay, but I don't want to risk getting stopped if you are driving since you are still on probation."

"Makes good sense to me. Hey! You don't like my driving?"

"You drive the truck like you drive the Sea Doo – fast and furiously."

"I learned on my Dad's truck. Yours is like a freaking Cadillac compared to his."

We motored back to the boat, and as we made drinks to take to the upper deck, we both noticed some evening thunderstorms brewing. "We may not get to sit on the upper deck for long."

"Roger that. Hey, I just looked at my phone, my parents left a message. I'm going to give them a callback."

"Sure, no problem. I'll head topside and meet you there."

I took my drink and mounted the stairs. Some storms were getting close, and I enjoyed watching them build. About 10 minutes later, Kim joined me, and said,

"Hoo boy, those storms are getting close."

"If we see lightning close by, I'll have you take the drinks down and I'll cover the chairs and follow you." She nodded in agreement.

"How's the folks?" I asked.

"They're fine. I told them I was being held hostage on a boat with a sex fiend who had his way with me several times a day."

"How did they take that news?"

"They were surprisingly calm. Well, I did not describe my stay here in exactly those terms. But close. They perceived that I was on a boat with a man for some days. They said to say hello."

"Did you identify me by name? I don't need your Dad coming after me with a shotgun and machete."

"Only the first name, so the odds of him finding you are slim. Besides, he would use a .45 pistol and a K-Bar knife."

"How not comforting."

A quiet evening

We watched the storms getting closer as we sipped our drinks. The wind started to pick up, with the lightning getting closer. By mutual agreement, we closed down the upper deck and went down to the covered front deck. The rain started a few minutes later, and it was hard to talk, it was coming down so hard. We retreated further into the living room.

The boat rocked a little in the wind, jerking each time it reached the end of one of the dock lines. I turned on the TV to see if the local weather was on. It was not, so we flipped around and agreed on a sitcom involving some friends. I lay down on the sofa, with Kim spooning in front of me. With my arm around her, it was so relaxing, I soon involuntarily dozed off.

I woke with a start and looked around. Kim was curled up in the recliner, with a cup of something that smelled like cocoa and was reading a paperback book. The TV was off, and the lights adjusted so she could read, but it was otherwise dim. "How long was I out?" I asked groggily.

"About an hour, I guess. You were so relaxed, I hated moving. I found a book by that MacDonald guy you were telling me about. He's really good!"

"One of my favorites. What are you drinking?"

"I found some cocoa; do you want some?"

"Can I just have a little of yours?"

"Sure."

I sat up and stole a swig of her cocoa. She remained quiet and content, reading while I was waking up. "What do you want to do now?"

"We could either find a movie to watch or hit the sack. I could go either way."

"I vote for more sleep."

"Cool." She put the book down and headed to the back.

I closed up and locked the doors, turned out the lights, and made coffee for the morning. I went back and did those things everyone does to get ready for bed. When I got back to the master bedroom, she was in bed with a tee shirt on. She announced some options.

"I have rescheduled your cunnilingus tutorial to tomorrow. You may approach me for either snuggling and sleep or calm, relaxing sex. Or both. Do please consider that you have had sex at least twice today when making your decision."

"I'd say let's snuggle and then see what happens."

"I already know the result of that, but your wish is my command, Captain."

I got into bed, and we embraced on our sides facing each other, and kissed for a while. The lightning had passed, but it was still raining, and the boat rocked in the wind. It was very romantic. I ran my hands up and down her back, ass, and legs as she played with my chest hair and occasionally stroked my back. The situation was getting steamier by the minute, and before long she rose up and stripped off the tee shirt, revealing that she was naked under the shirt.

"If you're running out of clean underwear and trying to conserve, we can wash clothes tomorrow," I said innocently.

"I thought you liked me naked."

"I do. Very much."

She wiggled her hips against mine. "Is there a cucumber in your shorts or are you glad to see me?"

"Mmmm. I choose B. I like what your hand is doing."

"Shut up and kiss me. Then stick that thing in me before it gets sad and leaves."

I kissed her as requested, then rolled on top of her. In seconds, we were joined. A low sigh escaped her mouth as I started gently thrusting into her. Her hips answered every push.

"That's nice, Dirk."

"I aim to please."

For several minutes, we enjoyed the lazy sexual rhythms, gently caressing each other with an occasional wonderful deep kiss. It was very relaxing. Out of nowhere, she said, "I forgot to tell my Dad I was being defiled by an enlisted man."

"That's a former enlisted man, and a senior NCO at that. How do you think the Master Gunnery Sergeant would feel about that?"

"I think he would be glad it is you and not a 'snot-nosed officer' as he used to refer to them."

"Well, we're both just plain old airline pilots now, so socially he should be relieved. I also think defile is not the correct term. If I recall correctly, it was you who blew me on our first date."

"While that is technically accurate, it is not germane to this discussion. Remind me to tell you tomorrow about the talking to he gave me before I went to pilot training. Please try and focus on the task at hand."

"Yes, Ma'am."

After a few more minutes, the task became more urgent, and after a brief increase in the tempo, I felt the urge and came quickly. I groaned involuntarily as I shot cum deep within Kim. She stroked my hair and said, "There. That will help you sleep."

After kissing her in appreciation, I rolled off her and we cleaned up. Snuggling was in order after that, and we fell asleep to the sound of rain and the now gentle rocking of the boat.

Day Three at the Lake – Thursday

We awoke about the same time, and I stumbled to the galley to get the coffee going, then we both performed the morning routine. The coffee was done by the time I came out. Kim was in the living room looking out the windows at the lake, wearing another of my tee shirts and was barefoot. Her hair was brushed and pulled into a ponytail, and in the morning light, she looked lovely.

I went to her, kissed her on the neck, and said, "Good morning, girlfriend. Are you having coffee today?"

She turned to me with a smile. "Good morning, boyfriend. Yes, please."

I poured us each a mug, and we went to the front deck. The sky was clear, the temperature after the rain the previous night was pleasant, and the wind was almost calm. We sipped the coffee in silence for a while, admiring the marina morning.

It was time for Kim to start planning. She asked, "Today is Thursday, right? Are we still going home tomorrow?"

"Yes, if you want to stay until then."

"I do indeed. What's the game plan for today?"

"Since the weather is nice, I thought we would take the houseboat out and spend the day bobbing around on the lake. I still need to check the forecast to be sure the wind stays at an acceptable level."

"That sounds so cool! When will we leave?"

"How about after coffee? I'll make breakfast while we are on the lake."

She drained her cup. "Let's go!"

I laughed at her enthusiasm. "I'll put you in charge of listening to the weather forecast, and I'll start getting ready."

"I'm glad to do that but want to help get underway."

We went inside, and I turned on the NOAA weather radio for her to listen to the forecast. The weather was going to be good, so I started showing her how to get the boat going.

We went to the inside control console. "First, we turn on the bilge blower for at least five minutes before we crank any engine. That clears any gas fumes from the engine compartment. Then we go to the back deck, open the engine hatches, and physically look for leaks and liquids."

"So that part is kind of like doing a walk around of the plane?"

"Exactly." We went back and lifted the engine covers. All was well.

She then asked, "Do we disconnect all the ropes and stuff now?"

"It's good practice to get the engines going first, to make sure they start. I've seen guys disconnect from the dock and drift helplessly while they were cranking away on engines."

"That makes sense."

The five minutes of blower time elapsed, so we went back to the console. She helped me get the boat ready to leave the dock.

"One last, slow look at each side to make sure all is disconnected."

We did that together, then I asked her to unhook the last line. We were free of the dock.

"We'll maneuver out of the slip from topside." We went up to the upper console. The boat was stationary in the slip, the wind calm. I showed her the button to push so the upper controls would take over. After making sure there was no traffic behind us, I gave the backing signal on the horn and eased both engines into reverse. The big boat slowly started backing out. A huge grin appeared on her face.

"This is so cool!"

I shared her enthusiasm. Alternating the engine controls, I put one in forward and the other in reverse to get us aimed out of the fairway between docks. Showing her how it worked, we eased over to the fuel dock. "Might as well get the waste tank pumped out, that way we don't have to be on a schedule to get back later."

"Makes sense. I was wondering what happened when I flushed the toilet. Head, I mean."

I carefully pulled up to the fuel dock, and as I approached, I saw the same two teenagers that were there yesterday. I looked at Kim. "Just asking, do you have underwear on?"

"I'll check." She lifted the tee shirt, revealing another bright but skimpy bikini. "Yep! I'm dressed!" she said with a grin. I just shook my head. Crazy fighter pilot chicks.

The kids tied us up to the fuel dock, and we went down and shut off the engines.

"Hi Dirk, Hi Kim! What can we do for you today?" they asked cheerfully.

"Hi, guys. Just a pump out and we may as well top off the Sea Doo if the hose reaches."

"You got it! Did you have fun riding the Sea Doo yesterday?"

They had no idea how fun our jet ski trip was. Kim said, "It was very enjoyable. Did you enjoy it, Dirk?" She asked innocently.

"Yes, I did. Very much." We looked at each other and smiled.

The kids went about the servicing tasks, and after 15 minutes or so, we were ready to cast off. I had Kim start the engines and I gave the high sign for the kids to undo the lines. We drifted slowly away from the dock, and once again went topside to maneuver. This time I had Kim operate the controls under my tutelage. She had a question.

"Why aren't we using the steering wheel to turn?"

"For maneuvering in the harbor, it's easier and more accurate to use differential thrust. Once we are clear, we'll use the wheel. You'll see why."

Going for a cruise

I got us aimed at the main part of the lake, and Kim started steering using the wheel. I had her push the engines up to cruising RPM, and we started cruising at a stately four or five knots. After she had us in the main part of the lake, I indicated the course to follow. "Steer for that point out there." She nodded understanding. "I'm going below to make breakfast. Don't run into anything, and if you need me, beep the horn." I showed her the button and went down the stairs.

I made my signature sausage and fried egg with cheese on hamburger bun sandwiches, peeking out the front windows every now and then to make sure we were not headed for a collision. I carried them upstairs and saw she had removed the tee shirt and indeed had the top and bottom of a swimsuit on. She was also wearing a big grin as she enjoyed driving the boat. "This is fun!"

We pulled the engines to neutral and then shut them off as we drifted down the lake, eating breakfast as we sat on lounge chairs, admiring the lake and scenery. It was peaceful and pleasant. After finishing our meal, Kim gathered up the plates, went downstairs, and returned with coffee for each of us. She was still wanting to plan our day.

"What do we do now?"

"After coffee, we can crank back up and find a cove to pull into. There we can either beach the boat and set beach anchors or anchor out in the cove. Anchoring out is less of a pain in the ass. Then we swim, ride the Sea Doo, nap, sunbathe, read, drink, grill some burgers, nap again, and generally enjoy life."

"That sounds great."

I was pleased the scheduling officer in her did not have anything to add. We lingered over coffee, just bobbing along the lake. A few boats went by with the people waving, but lake traffic was very light. That's why I like working on the weekends during the summer, and enjoying quiet days off on the lake during the week while everyone else in Atlanta was working.

We fired back up and found a quiet cove. I dropped the big anchor about 150 feet offshore. We would swing a bit with the breeze, but it was safe enough for our short time there. We went back to lounging around, deciding after a while to swim next to the boat. I put a floating line off the back for something to hold onto, and we dove in.

After paddling around for a while, we climbed back onboard by the swim ladder off the back end. Still wet, she wanted to ride the Sea Doo, so we got the lifejackets, and I launched the thing with her on the seat.

With me holding on to a rope until the jet ski started, Kim went through the start sequence and soon had us at full speed racing around the cove and out into the lake. She was really good at high-energy turns, showing the skill that she used in flying the F-16. I hung on grimly and hoped that we would stay right side up. After a while, she returned us to the boat.

"Still back there, boomer? I haven't heard you scream like a little girl for several minutes now."

"I'm in a state of shock. Just pull up beside the swim platform and shut it off."

"Yes, boss!"

As the ski coasted up to the swim platform, I grabbed it and we were stationary. Then I surprised her by saying, "I'm signing you off for solo flight. You can take it around by yourself if you want."

"Wow, thanks! I think I will!"

I pushed her off, and she cranked it up and roared off. I began to wonder what the insurance deductible was on that jet ski and if I would ever see it in one piece again. I sat on the back deck and watched her playing in the cove, doing tight turns and jumping her own wake. I could see her big grin and ponytail flapping in the breeze from a distance and was glad she was enjoying herself.

After a while, she returned, and I coached her into getting the ski onto the rack. With that done, she took off her life jacket and came to give me a tight, wet hug, then tilted her head up for a kiss.

"That was fun, boomer! Thanks!"

"You are most welcome, and thanks for bringing it back unscathed. Here's a towel."

She sat down and toweled off while excitedly describing some of the maneuvers she performed. Then she wanted to get to the next activity.

"What's next, nap, sunbathing, or drinking?"

"Your choice."

"I know, we could knock out your cunnilingus tutorial, nap, sunbathe, then start drinking."

"That plan has merits."

"Especially since it has been over twelve hours since we have had sex, it is vital to accomplish an orgasm each."

"I agree, although there is some pressure to perform."

"Don't worry, I am an Air Force Instructor Pilot. You are safe in my hands. So, to speak." She giggled.

"You are truly a nutcase."

"Yes, but I can tell you adore me. Shall we do it on the upper deck or in the bedroom?"

"While it would be fun on the upper deck, there may be a problem with spectators, and I am shy."

"The bed it is. Hit the head and report back."

The tutorial

We both went to wash up, then met in bed. She was on top of the sheet propped up on some pillows on her back naked with her legs slightly spread when I got there. All I could say was, "Wow!"

"Thank you for that, now assume the position. I'm kind of worked up after the Sea Doo ride."

"Must be the vibration."

"Yes, I'm sure that's it. Start at will, and I will advise you on any necessary improvements to your technique."

"Yes, Ma'am."

She drew her knees up and opened her legs wider. It was a fantastic view. I knelt between her legs, spread her labia with my fingers, and stuck my tongue in her slit, and started working south to north and back again. Then I went up and worked the clit for a while, to the accompaniment of some moaning. I tried wrapping my tongue around like a straw and sucking on the clit that way. She had me change the shape of the tongue and roll it back and forth up and down the now erect clit. She liked that very much, as evidenced by more moaning. I moved down and put the probe into her vaginal vault and curled my tongue up as though trying to wiggle a finger from within. She liked that pretty well, too.

"Ah, that's good! Kind of go as far as you can inside, then curl it up again. Oh! That's it!" She gasped. I did that for a while, then worked my way back to the clit. She was moaning a lot now and her hips were squirming, with no forthcoming suggestions, so I figured I was doing well. I used a free hand to find her boobs and give the long nipples some love. That got a good reaction, so I pressed on.

After a few more minutes, she could stand no more. "Get on me, boomer, I'm ready to burst!" I happily mounted up and slid my cock in all the way with one long stroke.

"Ahhhhh!" she moaned as I hit bottom. I started a hard thrusting into her, and her hips bucked into mine wildly. Her hands went to my ass, pulling me in as deeply as she could. Then her back arched and a loud, guttural groan escaped her lips. She pulled my mouth to hers and kissed me, our tongues searching each other's mouths in a frenzy. I could take no more and felt the hot stream of cum start in my balls and shoot out into her throbbing pussy. We held that pose with her back arched, our hips joined pushing desperately into one another, her pussy pulsating and my cock shooting spasm after spasm of cum into her.

After about 10 heartbeats we collapsed together. I lay on top of her as she murmured softly into my ear, "Oh, Dirk. That was fantastic. Thank you. Thank you!"

I also told her how intense it was for me. After a couple of minutes, I rolled off her and picked up a cloth that she had prepositioned on the bedside table. We did some wiping up, then she folded herself into my arms with a contented sigh and possessively threw a leg across me as I stroked her hair and back.

I asked, "Nap time?"

"Mm-hmm. You deserve it. I'm signing you off for advanced oral sex techniques, with the limitation that those techniques only be performed on me."

"Duly noted. Next one to get up, please look outside and see if the anchor is holding."

"Crap, I forgot we are out on the lake. How cool."

We dozed off quickly. After a blissful period of rest, I awoke before her and slowly snuck out of bed. Carrying my now-dry suit, I walked to the front and looked out the window. The shore was still where it was when we started, so I surmised that the anchor was holding. I pulled on my suit and went out on the front deck. It was hot, peaceful, and still.

A pleasant afternoon

She came out yawning after about 15 minutes and plopped down into my lap, putting her arms around my neck as she nuzzled it. She kissed my neck a few times, then sat up and gave me one on the lips.

"Thanks! Are you getting mushy again?" I asked.

"Yep. I think I will be for the rest of the day. You screwed me into a really good mood."

"I am in a great mood also. How about I make us a drink and we will sit in the shade and look at the lake?"

"A most excellent idea. I will assist you."

It was a little early for bourbon, so I mixed some tequila into a margarita mix and poured it over a lot of ice into large, insulated tumblers. We toasted, then returned to the deck, after I checked that the generator was still pumping water. It was getting hotter, so I turned on the ceiling fan.

"How in the world can you afford this floating palace?" she asked as we sipped our drinks.

"It was a lucky deal. A 767 Captain I know was going through a divorce and put a ridiculously low value on this boat as one of his possessions prior to the marriage. The judge called bullshit on that and demanded that he sell it for that value or face a fine for contempt of court, falsifying claims, etc. We were flying back from Europe when he told me about it. He showed me some pictures, and I bought it sight unseen during the flight for about a third of its value. I wrote him a post-dated check, called the military credit union as soon as I landed, and got an appraiser out here the next day. The appraisal came in at what he claimed it was worth, and the credit union approved the loan the next day. I came out here after a few days and had to ask where it was, which was funny because I was the owner by then. Crazy!"

She laughed. "That's wild!"

"Yeah really. It was fully furnished and even had bottles of booze on the bar. I just brought out my clothes and toothbrush and moved in."

"I was wondering about the furnishing and decorations. It's nicely done."

"Must have been done by a prior wife."

Kim decided she wanted to lay in the sun for a little while, so we moved up to the upper deck, and I laid out a lounger for her. She stretched out and then asked me to put sunscreen on her shoulders. I sat next to her and applied the lotion, thinking this would have been very erotic if I had not been sexually spent just an hour before.

"Boomer? Unhook my strap for me, will you?"

"Gladly, fair maiden. Shall I remove your bottoms as well?"

"I don't know. Do you want me to get sunburn on my ass?"

"Forget I mentioned it. I'll be over in the shade, reading."

I sat in the shade and read, every now and then looking over at her in admiration. I had to shake my head. Was I getting into boyfriend mode? Was I getting attached? I hoped not, as I liked my life the way it was without attachment and commitment. Admittedly, it was lonely sometimes. It was hard to think of Kim as just another piece of ass. She was more like a friend, and that was dangerous. We would really have to be careful in the weeks ahead if we saw each other again after this four-and-a-half-day date. Would we see each other again? What would that be like? Were we caught up in fun at the lake and great sex?

I heard her say something, and I looked up. I realized I had not turned a page in 10 minutes and had been staring at the lake. "Boomer? I asked if you wanted to go back downstairs to the air conditioning for a while. I'm getting hot."

"Yeah, that's a good idea."

We went downstairs into the oasis of cool air. She said, "Oh, that feels nice. Where were you? You looked like you were a thousand miles away."

I smiled at her. "Just wool-gathering, I suppose."

She was on to me. She asked softly as she looked into my eyes, "Were you thinking of what to do about me after we go home?"

I pulled her into my arms. "I'm going to be straight with you. That's what I was thinking about, where we are going. Do we have a budding romance or is it just being friends and simulating the boyfriend/girlfriend thing? Having wonderful sex and a fun mini vacation on the lake is confusing the situation."

She smiled and said, "That's fair, I suppose. We have to be careful, like we talked about. That's what I was thinking about lying in the sun."

I pulled her closer and kissed her deeply. She protested. "Stop that, I'm all sweaty."

"I don't care."

"Well, you are not getting it again until tonight after I have had a shower."

"So, you're saying I'm going to get it again?"

"Damned right you are! Let's get another drink. Are you hungry yet? All this deep talk about relationships and shit is making me hungry."

I grilled some burgers, and we ate inside where it was cool. We decided to swim one more time, then take the boat back to the slip.

Since the cove was deserted except for us, she talked me into skinny dipping, so we frolicked in the water naked for a while. It was very refreshing. She came over for a hug and kiss one time, which we had to cut short as I was springing a boner. She gave it a nice rub for a minute, then ran up the ladder laughing. The sight of her naked, wet ass with a great tan line dripping water as she went up the ladder ahead of me was tantalizing. I waited a couple of minutes before following her up the ladder so my erection would subside.

She handed me a towel, looked at my crotch, and said helpfully, "Looks like the cold water helped your boner."

"Gee, thanks. There's a word for teasers like you, and it's not complimentary."

"I've heard it before, boomer! I've been called worse. Do we pull up the anchor now?"

"As I have tried to teach you, we start the engines first."

"Oh. Yeah. Right."

Back to the marina

We got the engines going, and Kim helped me pull the anchor, which is an onerous task. She was really strong for a woman, pulling hard on the anchor rope until the muddy thing was back on board. We went to the indoor console and Kim steered us out of the cove and headed back for the marina.

Arriving back at the marina, I went topside and relieved her of helmsman duty and worked us carefully back into the slip without bending anything. She was a great help getting the lines back on and hooking up the shore umbilicals. I had her kill the engines, shift to shore power, and kill the generator. She wiped the sweat from her forehead after we were back inside. "Man, that's a lot to do!"

"I'm glad you were here to help."

"Do your other girlfriends help like I do?"

"You keep asking these loaded questions. I'll say this once and for all time. You are the best first mate I have ever had."

"Thanks!"

I looked at her and felt I had to say something. I took her in my arms. "Kim, if you want details of who I have seen and if they have come out here, I don't mind being honest with you and telling you that. I'm not sure you want to hear that. Before I met you, I saw a lot of women. Whom I see, if anyone after this vacation is part of that serious relationship shit we are avoiding for the moment."

She looked serious. "Ah, Dirk. I don't know why I asked that in that way. It just slipped out. I know you are a free spirit and that's the way I like you. I am enjoying this boyfriend/ girlfriend romantic stuff. But... I also know we need to work out a plan of how often and even if we ever see each other again. Let's agree to be romantic until you throw me out at the curb at my apartment tomorrow. Then it's either continue it or not. There! I said that without crying."

I put a finger under her chin and tilted it to me, then kissed each eyelid and her nose. I held her close. "I like it when you are girly and serious about relationships. I'm on board with being romantic with you whenever we are together."

She was tall enough to look me in the eye without tilting her head back. "Good. Here's to temporary or trial romances." She made a brave, small smile. "Now get me a drink! I am emotionally worn out. Then we'll shower and have a nice night together."

"Yes, Ma'am!"

An intimate evening

I made drinks and we moved out to the front deck to cool off under the ceiling fan and we looked at the lake and watched the sky. We held hands without saying a word. Evening cumulonimbus clouds started popping up, and we both watched the fury of nature shape them into baby thunderstorms. Dusk fell, and as we watched the marina lights, the breeze stopped and it became very humid and sultry.

We moved to the bathroom and had a fun, slow, relaxing, and sudsy shower. She washed mine, and I washed hers. When she turned her back to me and lifted her hair so I could do her back, I almost lost my composure. It was so intimate and trusting, I felt emotional for a moment.

After, we helped each other towel off, and dressed in tee shirts and underwear. We relocated to the living room sofa, and I made a bag of microwave popcorn while she turned on the TV and looked for a movie to watch. After some discussion, we settled on a romantic movie that I was sure would have a happy ending. There were some major movie stars, so we thought it would be a good one. About ten minutes into it, we looked at each other. "I'm not liking this movie," she said frankly.

"I agree. Too bad."

"Well, I searched all the channels and that was the best choice. Do you have any movies here?"

I had to laugh. "I have some old John Wayne movies, some of my favorites."

"Hell, bring 'em out!"

She looked them over and settled on *Donavan's Reef*, a comedy about a rich lady coming to a small Pacific island and falling in love with John Wayne. We watched it with her curled up into my side with her legs drawn up as we sipped a drink and munched popcorn. I have always loved the movie, and she laughed at the appropriate parts and liked the ending.

"See! After a rocky start, they got together, and it all worked out. Kind of like us."

I groaned. "Only you could draw that conclusion. We did not have a rocky start; we had an explosively fabulous start. Now we are trying to figure out what to do. How is that similar?"

She was undeterred. "Boomer, you are being obstinate. The situations are similar."

I gave up and looked out the window. "How about a nightcap under the stars?"

We fixed one last drink and went upstairs. The thunderstorms were not close by, but we could see them. The breeze had come back up, so it was not so stifling hot. Sitting on the lounge chairs and looking at the sky, we enjoyed the evening. After a bit, she reached for my hand and said, "Take me to bed, Dirk."

We went downstairs, I locked up and made coffee for the morning and we got ready for bed. I got to bed after she did and was pleased and surprised to see her in a pretty negligee.

"Wow! You look great. Did you have that in your helmet bag all along?"

She laughed. "No, I saw it in the 'broad bin' a few days ago. I wanted to wear it for you for our last night on the boat. It's a little snug, so I just used the jacket part."

I admired her as she looked at me calmly. "That is having an effect on me."

She shook her head. "Boomer, everything has an effect on you. Feel free to join me."

She looked at me with a smile as I disrobed and climbed in. We embraced silently, caressed each other, and kissed occasionally. There was no hurry. We had gotten to know each other, and each responded to the other's stimulus.

Soon I was playing with her boobs and nipples as she stroked my rod. I put a hand on her pussy and played in her with my fingers searching for her favorite places. Sometimes she would gasp as I hit one of the hotspots. I kissed her from her neck down to her knees, with her moaning softly along the way. Coming back up to her boobs, I kissed them and the long nipples, ending up at her mouth.

Wordlessly, she pushed me onto my back and got on top of me. With her gentle hand guiding my cock, she put the head at the entrance to her pussy and waited. I waited also, and after a bit, she slowly slid down and impaled herself on my rock-hard dick until it was buried in her. She gasped as she ground her pelvis against mine, back and forth, seeking the sweet spot where the maximum stimulus was achieved. It felt incredible, and I slowly began to push up with my hips as she ground her cunt against me.

After a few minutes, she grasped my hands as her breathing changed and grew ragged. She then put her hands on my shoulders and bent down for a passionate kiss as her hair fell around our faces. This roused her even more, and I could tell from her movement and sounds that she was close to a sweet orgasm. I patiently kept up my thrusting, now caressing and kissing her tits and nipples, with the other hand on her ass, urging her on.

Then she threw her head back and moaned loudly as if her heart was breaking. Her hips went into overdrive, rocking madly against my pelvis, and she groaned deeply and loudly as the orgasm swept over her. I was right with her, as my balls sent a load of cum from my hard dick into her quivering pussy at almost the same moment. We clenched our pelvises together and held still as the waves of ecstasy went through us. After an interval, she collapsed onto me, kissing me wildly as she did so, then burying her face in my neck. I stroked her back and ass, touched her hair, and murmured gentle words into her ear.

After a few minutes of recovery, we came to our senses and wiped down what we could. We both visited the bathroom and came back for a wonderful snuggle and curled up together without saying a word. A few minutes later, she looked up at me and said sleepily, "Goodnight, boyfriend."

"Goodnight, girlfriend."

We were fast asleep in each other's arms in minutes.

Day four – Friday

We awoke about the same time and lay there looking into each other's eyes, slowly caressing each other. It was very sweet and intimate. I did not get a vibe that Kim wanted to have sex, so after an interval of that, I got up and started the coffee and we did our morning routines.

I was sitting on the front deck looking at the lake when she brought our coffee out, bent down, and kissed me warmly. She sat across from me and took my hand. "Good morning, boyfriend."

"Well, good morning girlfriend."

"That was a great session last night. You really know how to turn me on. Did I scream?"

This was a great morning after talk. I almost blushed. "We make a great team, and besides you did most of the work. No screaming, but some very authentic moaning. I'll work on the screaming part."

She smiled sweetly and sipped her coffee while looking at the lake. No words needed to be spoken, it was a delicious interlude of shared intimacy. I knew she was wanting to schedule some events. I decided to beat her to it.

"What would you like to do today?"

She looked at me with a gleam in her eyes. She was ready to get a schedule in the books.

"That depends on when we are heading home."

"I don't have a preference. Probably about 1600 or so, then we could either get dinner on the way to your place or get takeout and eat at your apartment. You could even choose to show off your domestic skills by cooking something."

She pondered this. "I'm on reserve Saturday, just don't know what time yet. What time is your trip Saturday?"

"The show time is about 1700, direct to Frankfurt and sit for a day, gets back Monday to ATL about 1500. It's the same sequence I did when I met you on Monday."

This required thought on her part. I could almost hear the gears turning.

"I agree with the 1600 departure from here this afternoon. Dinner TBD. If you like, you can stay at my apartment tonight and then go back to your condo in the morning, get your flight gear, and go to work."

"Aren't you sick of me yet?"

She smiled. "I can put up with you for one more night."

I had to laugh. "This is the longest first date ever!"

She frowned. "I think Monday was the first date. Starting Tuesday, you have kept me hostage here in this isolated location, where I have been abused sexually and mentally."

"I think that is a matter of perspective."

She laughed again. "Anyways, we will leave this afternoon on time. In the meantime, we can fish, have great sex, ride the Sea Doo one last time, and swim."

"Leave me time to clean up and get the boat put to bed, about an hour or so."

"You also have to feed me. When will that be, or are you trying to make me weak with hunger to enslave me?"

I said, "I can feed you anytime."

She looked thoughtful. "Okay. Sex first, then food. After that, we will accomplish the rest of the schedule."

"I thought riding the Sea Doo made you horny."

"And you were assuming that we would have sex only one time? Jeez, you need to be more confident." She stood up. "Finish your coffee and report to the bedroom. I want you to ride me hard this morning!"

I had to laugh. "You are something else!"

Morning workout

We picked up our cups and locked the doors. Meeting in the bedroom, she was already naked, standing by the bed. She unexpectedly grabbed me by the waist and threw me on the bed. She was really strong, and almost the same height as me. She had no problem manhandling me. "Get those shorts off, boomer! Time's a-wastin'!"

It's hard to deal with a crazy woman, so I complied, and then she pushed me back on the bed and started a warm-up by kneeling before me and taking my cock in her mouth. Needless to say, she caused an involuntary swelling of my dick and was quite pleased with herself.

I managed to say, "You could have saved time by just staying in bed this morning."

She looked up, with some saliva dripping from her chin. "Naah, that was romantic time. This is fuck your brains out time!"

I was hard enough in short order, and she wasted no time in mounting me and slipping my cock between her lips. I gave a push with my hips to seal the deal, and she slid down the length of my rod until our pelvises met. "Yeaahhh!" she called out loudly and started a great rocking of her pussy on my groin as I pushed up into her. Things were happening fast. I fondled her boobs and was playing with the nipples when she asked me to bite them a little. I did as she requested, and she moaned expressively.

We kept that up for a while, with her riding me straight up when she bent down for a passionate kiss while holding me by the shoulders. I had my hands on her waist, encouraging the motions and pulling her down deeply onto my cock with each movement of her hips. Then she wanted to change positions. "Get on me from behind, boomer!" she managed to gasp. She dismounted, spun around, and presented me with her cute ass sticking up in the air.

I scooted into position and pushed the head of my dick to her waiting lips. She rocked back impatiently, and soon I was deep within her, thrusting like mad as her hips pushed back against me. I placed my hands on her waist again and pulled her hard to me as I pushed in. She wanted more.

"Harder, boomer! I want it hard!"

I was happy to comply and gave it to her about as hard as I could, her ass cheeks making that fantastic slapping sound as I pounded away. Soon I was reaching critical mass and would be exploding soon. I reached around for her clit and gave it a tweak with one hand as I squeezed her nipples with the other. She was groaning loudly now, and we both reached orgasm at almost the same time, loudly and proudly.

I stopped pumping her and stayed deep within her as the few last spasms of cum sprayed deep into her. I was sweating from the exertion and noticed that she also had some sweat pooling in the small of her back. After a few minutes, I pulled out and collapsed on the bed.

She turned around and joined me, reaching for a cloth to wipe up as best she could. "Damn, boomer! We're gonna have to do laundry. We're running out of clean washcloths!"

I had to laugh as I lay panting on the bed. "That's a good problem to have!"

Kim was still breathing heavily as she lay up against me and put her arm across my chest. "Whew! Nice workout before breakfast! I enjoyed that!"

She was running her fingers through my chest hair. "Damn, you got us all sweaty, boomer! Now I have to rearrange the schedule to clean up."

"You have my most sincere apologies."

"That does not sound sincere at all. You can make it up to me by feeding me."

We got up and threw a few clothes on, and rummaged through the fridge to see what was readily available. We agreed on leftover burgers as brunch. Sitting on the deck again, we ate in companionable silence. Then she announced she was ready for some Sea Doo action.

We put the life jackets on, checked the fuel quantity, and decided we had enough for a medium-length ride. I suggested, "The fuel will last longer if we go slower." She was not impressed. Soon we were zipping along at high speed and maneuvering as though the entire German Luftwaffe was after us in a WWII dogfight. I hung on firmly and tried not to scream.

After a while, she pulled up to a quiet cove and beached the jet ski. "Hoo boy! That is some fun. Hop off, boomer! We'll swim a bit and I'll rinse off from your oversexed assault on my lily-white body."

I jumped off and replied. "All I heard was 'Harder, boomer, faster!' so I did my best to comply with your wishes, my nutty friend!"

"That's not a valid defense. A gentleman would not have shagged me that hard, even though I wanted it."

She disposed of her bikini quickly and splashed around for a while, as we both enjoyed the cool water. "Drop your trunks, boomer! It's skinny dipping time!"

I threw my suit on the Sea Doo and joined her in frolicking in the cool water.

"Come here and wash off my nether region, Sir!"

"I will gladly comply with your wishes!"

We rinsed each other off and kissed a little. I was so fucked out I could not have gotten it up with a crane. Floating lazily, we enjoyed the late morning. There was a bit more boat traffic, but none came into the cove. We enjoyed the lazy time in the water.

Putting our suits back on, she wanted me to drive back. I shrugged. She was content to put her arms around me and lay her head on my neck as I drove us sedately back to the marina. After we put the Sea Doo away, putting the cover on this time, it seemed like there was a taste of goodbye in the air. We put the life jackets away and straightened up the back deck.

We went down the dock with fishing poles and caught some bluegill or perch, depending on where you are from. Then, on the walk back to the boat while holding hands, she looked over at me, smiled, and said, "This vacation has been really nice, Dirk. I've enjoyed it."

I returned the smile. "I've enjoyed it, too."

We got back to the boat and she said, "We might as well shower and then pack up." We then shared a lovely, warm, and sudsy shower, taking our time. We even washed each other's hair. It was very sweet and intimate, but had that taste of goodbye I had sensed earlier.

Toweling off, I gathered the laundry and stuffed it into a garbage bag. There was an inordinate number of washcloths. Together, we changed the sheets and I added those to the laundry bag.

"Damn. Boomer! Those sheets look like ..."

"I know. If only they could talk." That got a laugh out of her.

She made a point of returning the negligee and other borrowed items to the broad bin. She asked if she could hang on to the John D. MacDonald paperback she had started, and I thought that was a good idea. I went topside and stowed the lounge chairs with her help. We both stood there for a minute, then she came and put her arm around me. I did the same. We stood for a minute, enjoying the time together.

Then it was time to close up. I turned the water heaters off, set the A/C, picked up the trash, and set the laundry bag on the deck. I decided the perishable items in the fridge would be okay until I returned on Monday. We stepped off the boat onto the dock.

She exclaimed, "I just noticed the name. It's the same as Travis McGee's boat in the MacDonald novel!"

"Yep. The Busted Flush. Although I did not win her in a poker game, it's eerily similar. A tribute to my childhood fictional hero. Long live Travis!"

She smiled, "Long live Travis! May he never be forgotten."

Back to the real world

We carried our burden to my truck, and I cranked up and headed back to Buford, GA, and then our homes. We rode in silence for a while, then I said, "If I'm staying the night at your place, I should stop by my condo and get an overnight bag." She agreed that was a sensible course of action, and about 40 minutes later, I pulled into my condo off I-85 in Norcross, GA. We went into the condo carrying the laundry bag, and she looked around while I made up an overnight kit.

Kim commented on my bachelor pad. "This looks like a man's place. Nicely decorated but masculine."

"It suits me. I don't need a lot of room."

"Let's sit on the sofa and kiss awhile."

She did not have to ask twice. I put on some smooth jazz music, and we enjoyed kissing on the sofa. Then she said. "Can I see the bedroom?"

"Of course." I hoped I had made the bed before I had left. I had. Whew.

We climbed the stairs to the master suite, and she again looked around. "Let's lay on the bed and kiss for a while." I could not think of any objection, and we engaged in that pleasant activity for several minutes.

"Mmmm. Can I stay over at your place sometime?"

"I think that can be arranged, as long as you don't scream and scare the neighbors."

"You're a pig." Then she kissed me again. "Okay, let's hit the road, boomer. I need to check my schedule."

We got back in the truck, and she assured me that parking near her apartment would be readily available at that time of day. That was true, and after a 15-minute drive, we were soon at her apartment. She threw the contents of her helmet bag in the washer and went to her computer to pull up her schedule. She frowned in concentration as she entered the several dozen keystrokes needed to look into the airline's scheduling system. "Nothing yet, just early reserve duty in the morning," she announced. Kim would be on standby duty until the airline found an assignment for her but would be on call from 0400.

She signed off, and I signed in using her computer and confirmed my schedule. No changes.

We sat down next to each other on the sofa and pulled out printed copies of our monthly schedules and compared them. We would not have days off at the same time for the rest of the bid period, almost a calendar month. It looked like we would not be together for a while. We pondered that in silence for a while.

"What do you want to do about dinner?" I asked.

"Since I don't have any actual food besides frozen pizza rolls, saltine crackers, and canned soup, we could walk to one of many fine establishments nearby. My treat since you sponsored me on the boat."

I looked at her, smiling. "Let's go to the Ethiopian place we went the first night, on our first date."

She dimpled. "That would be splendiferous. Come here for a minute."

I did, and we kissed standing up for a while, with our hands roaming each other's bodies. She broke off and said, "Okay! Time to eat or you will be shagging me again."

"I'd rather do that than eat."

"A girl needs sustenance, boomer! Let me get my girly purse and let's go."

We walked to the restaurant, hand in hand. The greeter at the restaurant smiled as she seated us, admiring our loving attentiveness. We were the epitome of a couple in love. Were we? I asked the question after the server left.

"Are we still in the fuck each other's brains out phase, or is this the romance and love phase?"

"Yes, you dork, the first thing. I have many hormones raging through my body, but as you have so sagely advised, have attributed those thoughts to sex mania and not love."

"Ah, I see," I said sagely.

"No. you don't. You are thinking about carnal satisfaction while we women think about love."

"Men think about love, too," I said innocently.

"Oh yeah? What were you thinking about just then with that grin on your face?"

I had to laugh. "Your ankles crossed behind my neck as I was doing you."

She blushed. "See? That's all you men think about."

"Not true! Sometimes we talk about flying."

With that, we talked pilot talk about the airline, the differences in the airplanes we flew, the union, the contract, and the usual crap. I looked at her as the food arrived.

"I've never been able to talk aviation with a girlfriend."

"Am I still a girlfriend? For how long? Until you leave in the morning?"

I looked at her for a long time. "I'd say we are boyfriend and girlfriend every time we are together."

"I'd like that. How often will we be playing those roles?"

I pondered that for a minute. "I'd say we can get together for mini vacations, schedules permitting for the rest of the summer, then work out a visitation schedule for the winter."

She reached for my hand. "I'd like that, honey."

"I like it when you call me that."

"Don't get too used to it. I'm going to screw you tonight then throw you out in the early morning."

"I look forward to your attentions and will relish in the scraps of your love, my dear."

She laughed. "Oh, boomer. You are so full of shit."

A nice evening at Kim's apartment

We finished our dinner and strolled back to her apartment. It was pleasant, romantic, and otherwise pleasurable. I'm sure to observers that we were a couple in love. Were we?

Entering her apartment, she tossed the wash into the dryer, and I roamed her small living room, looking around and eventually finding some music to put on. Her phone rang, and she engaged in a conversation with our airline crew scheduling to negotiate a trip tomorrow. She hung up and said, "A Miami turn and that's it for tomorrow. Noon show time."

"Better than a 0400 wake-up to go to Buffalo."

"Yes indeedy. And ... we get to sleep in a little."

"Even better. I'm going to be flying all night. You'd better be gentle with me."

She smiled. "Of course."

We plopped down on the couch, calculated our FAA-mandated alcohol-free period then decided on a nightcap. Her liquor stocks were pitiful compared to the boat, so we had a fruity something and I popped some popcorn to munch while she looked for a movie. She curled up into me as I put an arm around her as we watched some chick flick on a cable channel. It was very romantic until the dryer buzzed, and she got up to fold her laundry. I got up and helped her get her uniform ready for work with the nametag, wings, epaulets, and other stuff then we settled in with the movie. It was very comfortable as if we had known each other forever instead of five days of vacation and partying.

The movie ended as expected, and we picked up and then got ready for bed. We met in her bedroom, where she had on a filmy light green sexy nighty worthy of a lingerie catalog. My groin was waking up. I exclaimed, "Wow! Two nights in a row, what have I done to deserve this?"

"Put a lid on it, boomer. I wanted the last night of our protracted date to be special."

I was immediately apologetic. "I'm sorry, Kim. You look fantastic. That color makes your eyes pop."

"Thanks. Now shut up and kiss me."

I did, and we fell back on her bed and enjoyed some heavy kissing and caressing. After some time passed, she said, "It's time to make love." I realized there was some finality to the act and gave all my attention to the act of love. She shed the nighty and after a long, pleasant time of foreplay, we were together again, naked. She pulled me on top of her. Soon, we were joined as one, and in a slow, sexy rhythm began a long, passionate coupling. After a long time, her moans became louder and closer together, and I knew that we would be joining each other in a sweet orgasm.

Our breathing came faster, and as one we increased our urgency toward the common goal. Faster and faster, we moved as one and pushed our pelvises together, each answering the other, until our frantic thrusting reached a crescendo. Moaning loudly, we each reached nirvana at the same time and pushed together until her pussy stopped pulsating, and my cock stopped spurting spasm after spasm of love juice deep into her loins.

We lay together, spent. Her hands ran through my hair. She whispered softly, "Oh, Dirk. Oh, Dirk." She stopped short of saying she loved me, but I knew instinctively that was what she wanted to say. I wanted to say it too but was afraid of making a commitment that I could not fulfill.

After a few minutes, I rolled off her and she went to get a washcloth. "We seem to go through a lot of these!" she laughed as we wiped up the mess from lovemaking. After a brief period of snuggling, we fell asleep in each other's arms. Would it be the last time?

Back to the real world

We awoke at the same time, and after visiting the bathroom, she said, "How about a last shower together? For this vacation, anyway." She quickly corrected herself. That sounded great, and soon we were once again sudsy and warm under the water. I'm not sure how I would feel in the shower alone after a week of this kind of fun. We gently washed each other, and ended up in an embrace, arms around each other while deeply kissing. My body responded as you would expect, and she could feel my erection against her belly. She reached down without breaking our extended kiss and stroked my dick. It felt wonderful. Then she did something totally unexpected.

Being about my height, she raised up on her tiptoes and guided me into her pussy. I stooped down a little, and it all fit nicely. What an incredible feeling, a fragrant, soapy embrace, with our skin slippery against each other while I was buried inside her! She put her arms back around me, and we stood there for a minute, intimately joined, and standing motionless while our tongues explored each other's mouths. I started a slow-motion pushing, and she responded, then said, "This is fun, but let's do this the right way on the bed, Dirk. It may be our last time for a while."

I agreed, and after pulling out, we got out and toweled off in record time. We lay on the bed together, and she pulled me to her. Our lovemaking was slow and sweet, but we were both energized by the sexy shower and quite worked up. Soon, we felt the urgency of a building climax and both came in a wonderful wave of euphoria. We kissed as I lay on top of her, still inside her. After a bit, I tore myself away from her and we went to the bathroom together to clean up. She looked at me with a smile.

"That was nice, Dirk. We work well together. You can really push my buttons!"

"I loved it! And you get me cranked up, too."

She reached up and put a hand on my cheek. "I should probably throw you out now and get ready for work."

"I can see I've worn out my welcome."

She laughed. "Get dressed, you dork. I'll see you out."

With that, I gathered up my overnight items and put clean clothes on. When I came out, she had a tank top and shorts on, was barefoot, and was in the kitchen. She said, "I am incredibly unprepared for serving breakfast to you! I don't have so much as a pop tart, and no coffee. You must think I am a terrible hostess!"

"I have no complaints. The hospitality has been incredible."

She smiled at that. I went to the door and set my bag down. She came to me and took both of my hands and looked me in the eye. We both started to speak at the same time.

"Well..." We both laughed.

"You first, boomer."

"No, you first."

"I was going to say that I really enjoyed our vacation together. I'm glad we know each other now. I'm just not sure ..." She hesitated, and her voice caught. A tear appeared in her eyes.

I said, "I know. It was fantastic. What we should do now is give it some time, stay in touch, and then do normal things."

She looked at me and nodded with her lip quivering. I held her close. I was close to crying as well. I stroked her back and hair as she clung to me.

"Hey, honey. It's going to be all right."

She smiled through her tears. "I like it when you call me that." She sniffled. "Big, tough fighter pilot, right?"

"Kim, you're all woman. That's the way I like you."

She gave me a salty kiss. "Goodbye, boyfriend."

"It's not goodbye, girlfriend. It's so long for a while."

With that, I released her and picked up my bag. She opened the door, and I stepped through. It shut behind me as I walked to the stairs. A wave of emotion swept over me. I found my truck and don't remember much about the drive home.

Mechanically, I went through the steps of getting ready for a trip and then took a nap for the all-night flight. When I got up, I decided not to take a shower, so I could enjoy her sweet scent on me that much longer. How corny. I'm never corny. I left on time and decided to use the employee parking lot at the airport instead of the MARTA train. I'm not sure why.

As I walked through the terminal, I felt something different and then realized I was walking by myself with no one holding my hand for the first time in days. I shook my head, angry at myself. Damn, Dirk! You need to snap out of this, man! You are acting like a love-sick teenager. Let's get down to the business of flying!

I went through the crowded security checkpoint using the crewmember lane. The security agent was jovial and friendly. I tried to be. "Hey, sir! Where you off to today?"

"Germany for the weekend!"

He laughed. "I was there in the Army. Better watch out for them Frauleins!"

I assured him I would and headed for our operations center. I signed in early, and read the usual management drivel emails, deleting as I went. After visiting with some pilots I knew, I went to the bag room and got out my flight kit from the hundreds of bags there.

The next stop was my mailbox, actually a cubbyhole among hundreds. I pulled out a week's worth of company and union crap, several envelopes of navigation chart changes, and a plain manila envelope with my name on it, scrawled in a feminine script. I opened the envelope, and saw a smaller one inside, again with my name on it, but the name Kim in the upper left corner. Under my name was the phrase, "Open after your flight when you are alone." She had left me a note when she came through operations at noon, three hours ago.

Maybe it was a dear John letter. I did not have time to look at it, so I went to the departure gate.

There I greeted the gate agent, who checked my ID against the flight authorization and let me down the jetway. Once at the entry door, I saw the Purser, an attractive flight attendant in her 40s who greeted me warmly! "Hi! I'm Debbie. I'm your Purser for the trip."

I introduced myself, then turned left and made my work area on the flight deck ready. I then went to walk around the outside of the big Boeing 767, looking her over carefully for our trans-Atlantic flight. Everything was fine, so I made my way back to the cockpit. On the flight deck, the Captain was there, and we exchanged greetings and pleasantries. I was flying with Jim all month. He was a good dude.

"Dirk, how were your days off? Do anything fun?"

I had to smile. "Went to the lake with a friend. It was great."

We then got down to work. After comparing the airplane logbook against the dispatch paperwork and talking over the weather enroute and in Germany, we started programming the navigation system for the flight. After, we did the 'Preflight' and 'Before Start' checklists, then waited for the door to close and the final paperwork as the passengers shuffled aboard.

The gate agent came up, gave us the headcount and the final paperwork, and as we felt the door slam we settled into the business of getting an intercontinental airplane out of Atlanta at rush hour.

About four hours later, we were in cruise flight at 33,000 feet over the dark, cold Atlantic. It was early morning local time, even though our watches said 10:40 pm. We had been routed farther north than normal, up over Greenland which was unusual. In the darkened cockpit, we could see the fringes of the Northern Lights to the north of our route.

The air was calm, the ride good, and the radio was quiet. The autopilot was on, the systems status page was blank, and when I tilted my head up to look at the fuel panel, the tanks were feeding normally.

I had just made a position report to air traffic control and checked the fuel supply, all was well. Jim had his map light on, looking at the union magazine. He and the airplane could do without me for a brief moment.

I could not stand it any longer and pulled Kim's note out of my kit bag and opened it. It was handwritten and read:

Dearest Dirk,

I wanted to thank you again for an extremely pleasant and fun week. Sorry to drop a note in your mailbox, I really am not a stalker!

I really embraced the role of your girlfriend, and even though that may have been premature, I loved it! I feel so natural with you, just so comfortable.

But ... My feelings are all over the place, and I'm actually glad we will not be able to spend any time together for the rest of the month so our libidos can calm down.

Let's stay in touch and work through the next steps, probably next month. I hope we can spend some time together at whatever level of relationship we end up in.

Call me when you get back to Atlanta, please.

Your sometimes girlfriend,

Kim

P.S. I know you could not wait to get to Germany to open this. Get back to work, Boomer!!!

I had to laugh at the postscript. There was a smiley face after her name, which was so Kim. I read it again, then turned out my map light and looked out at the night sky at the stars and the Northern Lights, lost in my thoughts as the airliner hurtled eastbound towards Europe.

Don't miss out!

Visit the website below and you can sign up to receive emails whenever Dirk Caldwell publishes a new book. There's no charge and no obligation.

https://books2read.com/r/B-A-UHDZ-FHULC

BOOKS2READ

Connecting independent readers to independent writers.

---

1. https://books2read.com/u/bre5JZ

2. https://books2read.com/u/bre5JZ

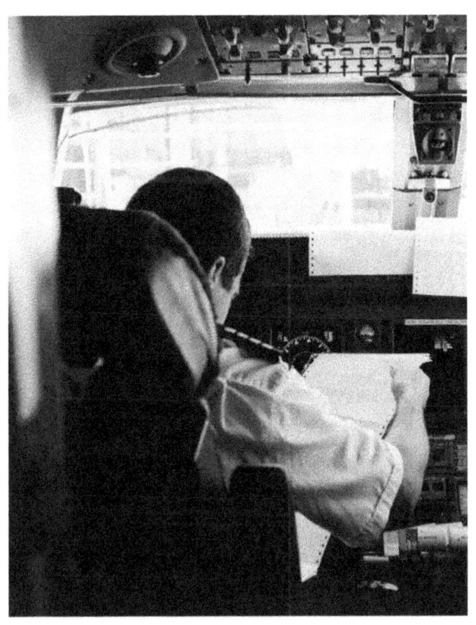

About the Author

Dirk Caldwell is the pen name of the author of an erotic book series. Dirk embodies the life experiences of the author as an Air Force veteran and commercial airline pilot. Most of the content is true and relates to the author's experiences. It's up to the reader to decide what is fiction and what is true life.